DESTROY ME GENTLY, PLEASE

Destroy Me Gently, Please

Please

Stories

Max Talley

Cover painting by Max Talley
Cover design by Kim Richardson
Exterior format by Jacob Arms

Published by Serving House Books
Lawrence Landing Company
Raleigh, North Carolina 27609
United States of America
www.servinghousebooks.com

Serving House Books is a proud member of

Independent Book Publishers Association
 and
Community of Literary Magazines and Presses

Paperback ISBN: 9781947175877
Library of Congress Control Number: 2025937474

SERVING HOUSE BOOKS

CONTENTS

"We are funny creatures. We don't see the stars as they are, so why do we love them? They are not small gold objects, but endless fire."

—Saul Bellow

Acknowledgments

– for stories first published in:

Whiskey Tit: "Paseo Tranquillo"
Works Progress: "Life's a Gas"
The Saturday Evening Post: "Ruby of Hesperia"
Abandon Journal: "Big Sur Impossible"
The Opiate: "Dishevel Me"
Chariot Press: "Internal Drive"
Iron Horse Literary Review: "Make That a Double"
Syncopation Literary Review: "Men of Good Fortune"
About Place Journal: "Almost Grand Junction"
Fiction Southeast: "If You Can Just Get Across"
Gold Man Review: "Longer Boats"
Litro: "Shipwrecked on Shiprock"

LEAVING CRAWFORD

Megyn Griffin relished her early mornings at the front desk before guests wandered in for breakfast. She could gaze out toward the rolling hills and await the rumble and horn blats from the first train of the day. Many more followed, masked by traffic noise, but the first brought everything back into focus: another morning in Crawford, Arizona. Situated right off I-40, it sat just west of Williams. While that little city had dubbed itself the "Gateway to the Grand Canyon," their old-fashioned downtown bustling with tourists, Crawford, on the other hand, was the "Gateway to the Gateway." Smaller by half, it relied on visitors who preferred lower rates and less kitsch, and the dazed interstate drivers who could not endure another highway mile without rest.

Coffee vapors steamed up around her face as Megyn studied a science book, aware that she was eighteen and a year behind on college plans. The delay? Her mother needed help to run the Mountain View Motel.

A stern biker deposited his metal sand bucket ashtray by the office's desk. "See you next trip, young lady." He headed for the raven-haired woman waiting on the back of his Harley.

Megyn *was* a young lady in Crawford. Maybe seventy teenagers, several dozen folks in their thirties or forties, and the majority of the population ranging from age sixty to death.

She mouthed pleasantries to the guests checking-out, consciously skipping the free continental breakfast of spotted bananas, Wonder Bread with butter pads, and sweaty gray sausages lounging in a metal serving tray.

Their utility guy came inside to stamp his feet. Still chilly in early April, dirty crusted snow on sidewalks, while larger pristine patches flecked green mountains in the distance. "Hey, Meg." The steam of his outdoor breath dissipated in the heated interior. Brandon Carter was twenty, handsome, and a complete fool. Megyn had known him most of her life. Attended school together, made-out once three years ago, but she'd moved on. Megyn planned to go to college, then become a teacher or a nurse in a big city, while Brandon held delusions of Hollywood stardom.

Due to the scarcity of others in their age range, and since both were considered attractive, every Crawford adult had asked, "When are you two kids going to get together?" The gossip-starved neighbors were desperate to live vicariously through them. Megyn shrugged it off and only Brandon's continued eagerness bothered her.

"Thought about my proposal?" He yanked at his jacket, shaking off the cold.

Megyn laughed. "You were joking, right?" She slapped the guest book shut. Despite a computer in the back, they still signed travelers in by hand. "I'm too young."

"I meant engagement for a year or two first."

"Not getting married until I'm thirty, or near."

Brandon lifted his baseball cap off then pressed it back on in frustration. "But it looks good on paper. Everyone says I'm the hottest guy in town, and when your braces are off, you'll be maybe the sweetest girl around." His face soured when she laughed. "Why didn't you get your teeth fixed before?"

"They got really crooked at sixteen." She eyed him. "What's your big rush anyway?"

"When I make it in Hollywood, I should have a wife. To seem regular to the public."

"Seriously?" She snorted. "The answer is no." Megyn switched to business mode. "There's a toilet clog in unit seven."

He kicked a cowboy boot against the base of the office desk in frustration.

"Dude, please chill." Megyn went to wipe down tables in the cramped dining area. "Anyways, everyone knows you're seeing the hag."

"Don't call her that," Brandon said. "Wendy Haggerty, and she's only fifty."

Megyn didn't reply since fifty hit folks harder in the southwest. The spring winds, dust storms, and sunny, dry-ass climate were brutal. Another reason she planned to bail. People needed moisture, to sweat, have oil in their pores, or they'd wither and wrinkle away. Cigarettes didn't help Crawford residents look young either. So, a small population of baby-faced youths existed amongst grizzled elders with tales of the good old factory days. Megyn knew nothing of the factory, beyond that its demise had left a wake of bitter, desolate souls forever mumbling about it. Crawford was a ghost town in the making, haunted by humans in denial of the end being in plain sight.

"I'd drop Wendy the minute you agree." Brandon waited for her reaction. "I was planning to end things soon anyways."

Megyn turned from cleaning. "As if you're calling the shots."

He grabbed the toilet plunger from behind the desk. "When you see my face on that billboard west of town, you'll be sorry." Brandon slammed the door behind him.

Megyn collected the departing guests' key cards. She was viewing colleges in Colorado on her laptop when the door bells jingled.

"Is it noon already, Mom?"

"Call me Candy," her mother said. "I might be near fifty but I plan to remarry. Best not to reveal attachments right off."

"Wow, I'm an attachment now." Megyn gazed up from her screen. "You'd have to move to Flagstaff to meet anyone decent." Her father died seven years ago at age forty-eight. Possibly cancer from working at the chemical plant in Joseph City. Candy wouldn't talk about it. The settlement paid off the motel, and that closed the book for her.

"There's eligible men around." Candy sighed. "I'd just need to lose twenty pounds, get my hair done," she stared outside, "and drive over to Ash Fork for weekly facials." She shuddered. "I look older than my age."

"No you don't, *Candy*." Megyn hugged her mother, who often needed reassurance. "And stay away from Vern's Beauty Salon. She does permanent makeup stuff and gives brutal acid skin peels she isn't trained for."

"Vern told me she has a cosmeceutical license."

"Bet I can print you one of those from the internet right now." She gathered her laptop, coffee mug, and books. Her mother worked noon to seven, then Megyn spelled her until the front desk closed at ten p.m. On Sundays and Mondays, her high school friend Skyler stepped-in so Megyn could have two days off.

Not in a rush to do anything, Megyn slumped on the iron furniture set on the office's porch. The sun shone and it felt warm, but she kept her lined blue jean jacket fastened. High in the pine-covered mountains, they got some water from the snowmelt. It might hit 90 in the summer, but never the 110 degree hell of the arid plains and desert surrounding Phoenix.

When the familiar sputter and hum of a vintage Ford F-1 pickup approached, she didn't have to look up.

"Hey, young lady. Need a ride? Not that there's anywhere to go in this godforsaken shithole."

Cole Jepson, the only local that Megyn admired. Tragic, him being fifty-six, but she'd adopted him as her uncle. His hair a wild tangle, thick and graying, with a gritty beard sprouting on his chin. He looked pummeled by life, but had once been something. Blue eyes still clear and boyish despite the weathered face. The fact that his book of poetry was published by a New York publisher in his thirties was what impressed Megyn. Crawford didn't have celebrities, but he was a notable person. Educated. Spoke in clear sentences.

"Sure." She hopped in. "Take me to the DQ." Across the railroad tracks lay the derelict east side of town, with mostly shuttered businesses and tumble-down homes. Leftover reminders of Crawford's past.

They reached the Dairy Queen's deserted lot and Cole parked. Megyn stared at the hollow structure, the frame and insignia still there. She could close her eyes and imagine the ice cream flavors, being driven over by her mother when she was younger. "It's so weird," she said, "to feel nostalgia when you're still a teen."

Cole laughed, pushing a mess of hair back from his brow. "Never cared for it myself." He squinted toward a barren, weedy patch of land with a damaged screen rising above it. "I do miss the drive-in though. That was a blast, back in the day."

"I barely remember it. Closed when I was ten, I think."

"But you've been there since then..."

The abandoned parking lot served as a make-out spot for high school kids. "Well, maybe once or twice."

"Who can blame you?" He rustled around in his seat. "Hope you're still planning to—"

"Leave Crawford? Hell, yes," she said. "Waiting on three colleges. They send acceptances soon." Megyn noticed Cole's mouth twitch like he knew what she was about to ask.

"Why did you come back? I mean, New York City. You were published, gave readings, could have been a poetry teacher at Columbia or some liberal arts college." She gazed at him. "It kills me being here, and I'm not even nineteen."

"New York scared me," Cole replied. "I couldn't take it."

"You? You're not scared of anything." She shook her head. "I saw you bounce that mean drifter who wouldn't leave the Mountain View." She tapped his hand. "And when a steer got loose on Main Street. Who cleared it off? Not our useless sheriff."

"That's different." Cole played with an unlit cigarette. "I can deal with things, one on one. New York is filled with people, buildings, streets, cars and buses, voices crying out. Pent-up emotions and frustrations, and violence coming from everywhere." He raised his fists like a boxer. "I couldn't fight it. Sapped my energy." His head bowed. "Guess I'm a coward."

Megyn punched his shoulder hard. "You are not. Go write some new poems. I read your first book all the time. You have so much talent. Just need to get out of Crawford."

He coughed. "Nah, I'm a blown gasket."

"I am *not* listening." She cranked open the passenger door and jumped out. "I'm walking home from here."

"Hey, wait." He puttered the old Ford along beside her.

Megyn put on headphones and blasted the music. She waved Cole on ahead by the hulking closed factory. It once made wire hangers and metal hooks and nothing that made any sense to a teenager in the 21st century.

Brandon finished his duties by two p.m. Hammered window screens back into place, plunged two toilets, and added touch-up paint outside the motel units. Left him four hours to kill.

The Mountain View had created two-room suites in the smaller side of the L-shaped building. More expensive but they'd become popular. At six, Brandon served drinks in the outdoor patio area until seven-thirty.

Possibly illegal, but the local police chose not to interfere. Candy was trying to bring tourists into town, who would stay at motels, buy food at restaurants, overpriced gas, and be given parking and speeding tickets. It would be anti-business, against Crawford's survival to enforce the letter of the law. Brandon claimed to be twenty-one so he could bartend.

A Los Angeles film producer was staying in a suite, with two female assistants in the adjoining one. Yesterday, Simon Maybank told Brandon he had natural good looks and vaguely resembled a young Tom Cruise when he smiled. Simon wanted to talk more tonight after he returned from scouting film locations.

Brandon pressed Wendy Haggerty's number.

"You done for the day, slugger?" she asked.

"Yeah." He never knew what to say to her. "What's going on?"

Wendy laughed with a whiskey rasp. "Nothing. Be at the semi-trailer in thirty."

"Do we have to meet there?"

"We can't go to your parents' place, and Gil's around here," she said. "He might not walk anymore, but his hearing is good."

"Yeah, okay, I just thought—"

"We have to be discreet."

"Everybody in town knows, Wendy."

"See you soon."

At seventy-one, Gil Haggerty had suffered two strokes in the last years. The second requiring a wheelchair and an attendant to bathe him. Gil's wealth allowed his purchase of acreage on the north side of the interstate a decade ago. His initial plans to raise crops or keep livestock failed, due to the hilly terrain with dramatic rises and falls. Not good for planting, while cattle preferred to graze on level grassy fields.

Halfway up the highest rise of his property on the western border of Crawford sat a semi-trailer. The cargo compartment from an 18-wheeler Gil owned. Across its metallic flank, painted in seven foot letters was: *TRUMP 2024*. It had been propped there since it first read *2020*. In whatever direction one traveled on I-40, this mammoth container and its message were clearly visible.

Brandon drove his Toyota pickup along the winding tread that dead-ended behind the semi-trailer. He wet his dark hair back with bottled water, then knocked on the loading doors.

"It's open," Wendy yelled.

Inside lay a queen-sized mattress. A dim battery-powered lamp glowed while a boombox played maybe Whitney Houston or Mariah Carey. Brandon didn't know old pop music. Wendy was propped on an elbow in her underwear, drinking Jack Daniels from the bottle. "Let's get going."

Brandon stripped. Wendy Haggerty possessed a stunning figure, something out of 1950s films, curves jutting in every direction. Her body was legendary in town, provoking gasps and stares of wonder—even from young children. However, something happened to her face. The baby fat had drained away, highlighting her father's wide flat nose and her mother's lantern jaw. Now, her eyes appeared sunken into their sockets, and they showed a combination of rage and fear, as if aware they were sinking.

Brandon kneeled onto the mattress edge.

"Feel like talking first?"

Her face reddened. "Do locals call me... the hag?"

"Nobody says that, not around me." Just a white lie this time. Brandon reached a hand out to caress her.

"Don't!" She rolled over. "Okay, let's get going."

Brandon had been confused of late. Sure, he liked women, and planned to marry a normal pretty one, soon as Megyn agreed. But lately, he'd been watching cowboy movies on TCM while he worked. He wanted to know those rugged, lanky men, ride horses with them, share a bunkhouse. At present, he could stare at Wendy's shoulder blades and abstract it. He closed his eyes, imagining crisp blue jeans and shiny leather saddles.

"That's it?" Wendy craned her neck sideways. "Well, save the rest for your little girlfriend down at the Mountain View."

Brandon dressed quickly. "She's not my—"

"I don't care." Wendy covered herself with a sheet.

Brandon wandered out to the Toyota, blinded by the sudden blast of afternoon sunlight. The peak of his life; he deserved better.

Arriving at the Mountain View just before six, he put on a clean white shirt, a bolo tie, and a dark server's vest. Then he mixed drinks on the terrace fronting the motel's deluxe units.

The producer, Simon Maybank, entertained two older German couples on outdoor furniture padded with pillows. When the couples trekked off to Crawford's center for dinner, Simon beckoned Brandon over.

"Foreign investors," Simon whispered. "I'm always raising money. You know, films aren't cheap." He signaled his assistants and they retreated into their suite.

"So you're a producer?" Brandon sat at the edge of his seat, chest jutting forward.

"Producer, director, location scout." Simon studied Brandon while finishing a Vodka Collins. "And what's your plan?"

Brandon coughed. "I want to star in a franchise, like Harrison Ford did with *Indiana Jones*."

"Really? Who would your character be?"

Brandon flashed his dazzling smile. "Zack Bone, a gym coach by day, but after PE class, I put on a cowboy hat and become... Eldorado Bones." He glanced over for affirmation.

Simon winced, head tilted slightly. "You *did* go to high school and maybe Crawfish College, right?"

"I'm just turning twenty-one, but I graduated Ash Fork High last year, in the top 100% of my class."

Simon grinned. "It's getting dark. Why don't you clean up the bar then we'll talk in my room." He refilled his drink and vanished within.

Brandon rolled the bar cart on wheels across the main street, setting it back into the motel office. Megyn looked up from her studies and stifled a laugh at his outfit.

"I'm onto something," he said. "Listen, can we meet tomorrow?"

"Not another proposal." She rolled her eyes.

"No, just to hang out. Remember years ago, we'd watch the trains go by at sunset?"

"When you got me high and tried to—"

"No." He sighed. "I just wanted to talk like we used to do."

Megyn flattened her book open on the counter.

"Sure, okay. Nothing else going on."

Outside, Brandon primped in his Toyota's rearview mirror before knocking on Simon's suite.

"Come in." The producer reclined on his king bed, barefoot and wearing a silk bathrobe. "Make yourself comfortable." Four candles burned in the dimly lit room.

Brandon perched on a chair, keeping his chin thrust out, as he'd practiced.

"So this is how Hollywood works," Simon said. "You do extra parts, non-speaking, then you get a line, maybe two. If you move right and speak well, you could get a character role for some screen time." He paused. "With adventure scripts, the way in is as a stunt man. If you can survive flaming car crashes without sustaining heavy bodily damage, then you're a shoo-in for an action movie."

"I couldn't find any of your films on Google."

"Ever heard of *Fast and Furious?*"

"You produced those movies?"

"No, *Slick and Serious,* the knock-off series. Huge in Taiwan and Jakarta." Simon tugged at an earlobe. "Anyway, someone has to put in a good word for you. You do something for them and they help you out in return, right?"

"Yeah, I guess..."

"For instance, I could use a back massage." Simon untied his bathrobe.

Brandon turned away. He'd played sports and showered with the team, but never seen a man so pink and hairless—it confused him. Maybe Brandon just liked cowboys.

"What's the matter?"

Brandon shuffled toward the door. "I need to consider things."

"My card is on the table. Call me, but only when you're ready."

Megyn finished her shift all tangled-up. She had wanted to ask Cole to go sit atop the water tower at dusk and watch the first stars appear in the night sky. Cole had never acted weird with her since she turned eighteen, but what if he did? How would she gently say no without ruining their friendship? And what if she felt cold after sunset and leaned on him, giving him a signal. She *was* mixed-up and needed affection, or at least understanding in a decaying, lonely town. Cole might go along if she started something and that would be awful. Or he might fend her off and then she'd feel mortally insulted. Or worse, they might just sit there. So she couldn't ask him to join her, and yet there was no one else *to* ask. Skyler would only tag along if a beer or weed was involved. She didn't understand starlight, poetry, or anything important.

The door bells jingled at noon when Megyn expected her mother.

Instead, Cole stood there grinning. "Thought we could drive over to Ash Fork, get you lunch, and well, breakfast for me."

She moved her mouth around her braces. "I'm real busy with college stuff." She couldn't make eye contact. "Maybe it's best to skip our adventures this spring. Distracts me from studying." Megyn gazed up. Cole had already turned away, but she could tell by his sagging posture she'd hurt his feelings. The pickup truck's engine faded to the west, and she wiped away tears when Candy came to spell her.

"What's wrong, darling?" Candy embraced her. "Did Brandon Carter insult you? I will slap some ugly into that dumb-ass pretty boy."

"No." Megyn sniffled. "What if I get stuck here forever?" She didn't mention the rejection that came in the morning mail.

"You're almost nineteen and those three colleges will be fighting over you."

Megyn slept the whole afternoon then took a sick day the next morning. Imposed a 24-hour delay on Brandon's "let's hang out" plan, because who cared when they met? Every day felt the same in Crawford. A total bummer.

Just before six when Brandon was due, she ran west to the Grand Canyon Tavern. *Make things right.* The familiar vintage Ford sat parked just outside. Underage for a bar, she tapped on the frosted window of the historic tavern until she got Cole's attention.

He shuffled out, expression stern. "Never interrupt a man mid-beverage."

"Just wanted to talk for a sec."

"I brought something for you inside my truck."

Megyn slid into the passenger seat.

"Wrote this poem last night." He reached over her to the glove compartment. "Printed it out and everything."

She tucked the folded paper into her pants' back pocket. "Write ten more."

"Jesus. Tough lady."

Megyn set the door ajar, preparing to dash. "You know Skyler?"

"Of course. She's, what do they call it, your bestie, your BFF?"

"Nope. She's my girl, my pal." Megyn paused. "You're my bestie."

Cole seemed startled, then frowned. "Buzz Skagmeyer might not like that." He glanced toward the bar's window. "We been drinking together since long before you came around."

Megyn gave him the finger, smiling. Then she thumped the top of the pickup goodbye and went skipping back toward the Mountain View.

Brandon's Toyota waited by the motel units. The film people had checked-out so no bar set-up was propped outdoors. "Don't you look all happy," he said. "I thought you were sick yesterday. What, did Aunt Flo visit?" He laughed—alone.

"Let's go." She jumped in and turned on the radio. "Just so you know, we're not fooling around or nothing tonight."

"Damn, you think I've got a one-crack mind? Hey, truce, okay?"

"Sure."

Brandon parked near the strip of woods that bordered the railroad tracks. Trains ran hourly, except for a flurry between six and eight. He spread a blanket and unwrapped a tuna fish sandwich, then offered her half. He'd brought beers, but Megyn just wanted sips from his. The ground shook when a westbound cargo train rumbled by.

"We'll be better-off if McDonald's comes," he said. "Maybe an IHOP too. Then a train station to bring more tourists here from the Grand Canyon."

"We're twelve miles from Williams. They can't have stops in every little town." Brandon's bottle rim tasted of tuna but she didn't care. Made it feel like camping out, roughing it. "Anyway, you're going to Hollywood. Did that producer—"

"He gave me his card." Brandon stared away. "It's a weird world. But if I became a star, I'd come back to Crawford."

"Why?"

"To show everyone who thought I was a stupid loser that they were wrong."

"You want to be a movie star just for spite, to get back at people?"

"Yeah, of course." He swigged his beer. "But I'd buy land here too. Make improvements."

"A trailer-bed on every hillside?"

"Jesus, I'm trying to be for real tonight."

Megyn punched his arm softly. "You are." She finished eating.

Another horn sounded as an eastbound train approached. This one came slow, a jangle of ratcheting freight cars, the squeal of brakes. They watched it stagger along, passing them gradually. The line of boxy containers were rusty, discolored, graffiti-marked, and ugly as hell, but in that moment, the most beautiful thing Megyn had ever seen. She counted twenty cars. "I could walk along and keep up." And she did just that.

"Hey, where you going?" Brandon trailed behind her.

Megyn jogged faster then jumped up on the edge of an empty freight wagon. *So easy, so fun!*

"Get off there," Brandon shouted. "What about us?"

His words were soon drowned out by the rattle and locomotion. Leaving a stick figure waving his arms.

The train accelerated through the pine tree dusk until she couldn't see him anymore. The clanking give-and-take of section couplings and metal wheel tremble overwhelmed everything else. As the dazzle of starlight showed overhead, she felt euphoric, totally high. Three-hundred bucks lay scrunched in her purse. Not enough for anything of consequence, but whether practice or a dress rehearsal for her eventual escape, she'd ride it through to Flagstaff. A few days there to clear her head. Unfolding Cole's poem, Megyn squinted in the dying light. Just seventeen words.

Leaving Crawford:
Right away, damn it. Sooner.
Don't you ever come back! (Like I did...)
Not never.

PASEO TRANQUILLO

My father once told me, "Robert, life begins at forty." Unfortunately, Hank Weston died at fifty, soon after imparting that information—so I was unable to circle back for specifics. At present, I'm heading fast toward fifty-nine. Time is limited; there is no happily ever after, no forever stretching to the horizon. So roughly ten years of youthful activity lie ahead. My best life? I don't expect fireworks. I'll settle for a decent span of time with all original body parts. To visit restaurants and bars, to walk around foreign cities on my own two feet— alongside my wife.

"His name is Dudley Cragmile?" I asked Emma as we sipped a local Pinot Noir on our patio while surveying the vacant neighboring property. Crickets chirped at dusk, the sky lay streaked with pink.

"From near Phoenix," she replied. "Bought the place sight unseen, beyond Internet photos." She stretched her legs on the recliner. "Dudley sounds like a librarian or an accountant."

"Perfect," I said. "The whole point of us buying on Paseo Tranquillo was for the peace and quiet. Let's hope he's an introvert, a stamp collector."

Emma held out her glass. "Another splash, Rob?"

In 2017, before real estate prices skyrocketed, we found our two-bedroom home in Santa Valeria on California's south coast. Paseo Tranquillo is a quiet lane, lush with palm trees and tall pines. Our quarter-acre seems out of a dream in a neighborhood of nice old cottages. Days are sunny, then at night, sea breezes waft in to cool down the afternoon heat.

"Rob? Robert?" Emma prodded me after midnight in bed. "I think he's arrived."

"What? Oh." I rolled off the mattress half-awake then peered through our upstairs window. Due to tree branches and fencing, my view was limited. But a long car, like a Suburban, sat idling on the neighboring driveway. A man in a cap and sweatpants trundled back and forth, carrying boxes.

"Can't make out his features, but he's alone."

"No kids. Good," she mumbled. "Is he…?"

"White? Yes, I think so."

Emma kicked me from the bed. "That's not what I meant. Is he young or old?"

"A bit hunched with a wide stance," I replied. "I'd guess seventyish."

"Great," she said, then rolled over into immediate sleep.

Though Emma is fifty, through good genes, retaining baby fat in her cheeks, and monthly visits to a hair colorist, she's often mistaken for early forties. While I come from Irish and Welsh ancestry, where by middle age our lined faces mirror the craggy isles and jagged cliffs of the homelands. I just nod whenever someone announces how lucky I am to have such a young, vibrant wife. Only when I overheard her speaking by phone, "Well you know, I married a much older man," did I become slightly vexed.

At eight the next morning, I heard scraping, banging. I squinted across to see a U-Haul trailer and one of those metal storage PODS jutting into the street. After coffee and a muffin, I went to welcome Dudley to the community. Ignoring new neighbors is what causes unspoken tensions that can eventually rise to disputes. Not for me. Emma slept late since her shift at Santa Valeria Library began at eleven. I brought a croissant along as a housewarming gift.

"Good morning," I said loudly, in case he was hard of hearing. My plush bathrobe over pajama bottoms would peg me as a nearby resident.

"No reason to shout." He craned his neck, scowling, then continued unloading long slim boxes. *Fishing rods?*

"I'm Robert Weston, from next-door. Heard you arrive last night." I paused. Nothing. "Are you Dudley Cragmile?"

A heavy crate dropped to the asphalt. "Dutch," he said. "Dutch Cragmire." He winced. "Only Mama called me Dudley and she's long dead."

"Okay, Dutch." I extended the croissant, smiling.

His nose wrinkled as if I'd proffered a turd. "No thanks, Bobby."

"Uh, Robert is fine."

"Bobert."

"Do you need help moving any—"

"Nope."

"Well, I wanted to invite you to dinner sometime, as a welcome."

"You and me?" Dutch's face soured.

Then Emma strolled over in shorts and a white blouse. She looked much better than anyone had a right to after waking just fifteen minutes earlier. "Howdy, neighbor," she said, in the way only guileless people can pull off.

Dutch removed his cap, wiped sweat from his brow with the gaiter tied around his neck, and grinned wide. "Aren't you pretty," he said. "You Bobby's daughter?"

Emma laughed, then I laughed—cringing inside. "No, Robert's my husband." She crooked an arm through mine in a very satisfactory manner. "From Arizona, right?"

"Tell you about it at dinner. Bobert kindly invited me over." He glanced at me. "You meant tonight, right?"

I froze. Emma and I always pre-cleared dinner guests with each other.

"Yes, he did," she replied, discreetly elbowing me. "Come by at seven for a drink first."

Dutch ambled over to our patio that evening, gripping a bunch of flowers he presented to Emma. Dressed in military fatigues, he sprouted a bristly, grown-out crew-cut.

Emma set the flowers inside a vase then poured him a glass of red wine. "Your outfit. Were you in—"

"End of Vietnam," he said. "Fifty years ago."

"Thank you for your service," Emma said.

"Yes, thanks," I added. "Must have been a nightmare there."

Dutch scowled. "I regret all the hippie protesters and politicians that didn't let us finish our job. We could have nuked North Vietnam, wiped them off the map, set an example to show China we meant business."

Emma appeared stunned into silence.

"Interesting," I said. "Hey, there's a hummingbird by the feeder."

Thankfully, both Emma and I were moderate liberals, bolstering each other through monstrous presidents and backward-leaning religious extremists who'd commandeered the Supreme Court.

Dutch took a mouthful of wine until his cheeks bulged out, then spit it just off the patio. He eyed our startled faces. "That's what you're supposed to do at a wine tasting, right?"

"Yes," I said, "at a tasting."

Emma took a swig from her glass and spit it out with the gusto of a lumberjack on a payday bender. She winked at me, apparently trying to normalize it.

"I usually hate wine but this is kinda fun." Dutch raised his glass for a refill.

"Yes, yes." I tried to maintain control. "But we have dinner waiting inside."

"I brought a bottle of Early Times." He carried a liquor store's brown bag.

"Whiskey?" Emma said.

"Yup. Helps burn through the food." He smiled. "Overwhelms any flavor, good or bad."

"Uh, Emma only drinks beer and wine, and I'm recovering..." I struggled to fabricate something.

"He's recovering from liver damage last year," Emma quickly said, squeezing my hand.

"You do look a bit pale and sickly, Bobert." Dutch pressed his knuckles together. "Well, more for me then."

When he ate our fried chicken with his hands, Emma quickly picked up hers. So I joined in the caveman ritual too. "Are you a doctor, Dutch? This neighborhood has become so pricey to buy in."

"I'm retired," he said while chewing. "Pretty damn tasty." Dutch rubbed greasy fingers over his face. "Almost as good as Chick-fil-A. You guys must go to that local one a lot."

"Not so much." I gripped Emma's knee under the table for solidarity.

Dutch leaned back. "Retirement gives me more time for my research."

Our dinner eventually ended and by nine Dutch staggered back toward his property.

"Well, that was...something," Emma announced.

"We needed to break the ice," I replied. "Now we just wave in passing, say hi, and go on with our life." I picked a print off the floor. "Is this your photo of Gavin Newsom?"

She shook her head.

"Maybe Dutch dropped it. That's weird."

"He seemed to be staring at you during dinner, Rob."

"I know, and he was ogling you," I said. "I mean, men do that, but his mouth was practically hanging open."

Emma blushed. "He *was* in really good shape for a man in his seventies." She gazed off into the middle distance. "Too bad he's so raw and unfiltered, so January 6th. My friend Nancy loves well-toned, older men."

I kept silent, one hand resting on my burgeoning paunch. Part of what's called a "dad bod," though I'm not a father. Soon after marriage we decided the world was going to hell and maybe we weren't cut out to be parents.

"The way he kept calling you Bobert after you corrected him, and pronouncing it like Lauren Boebert." Emma winced. "Almost goading you." She massaged my tense shoulders.

"I need a cleanse for the whole evening."

Emma nodded. "You mean, Rachel Maddow?"

"Yes." I kissed her, then we nestled together on the living room couch to watch MSNBC.

Later in bed, while Emma hovered above me, she let her fingers play across my belly. "Have you thought about lifting weights again, doing sit-ups like you used to?"

"What?" I tried to maintain concentration.

"I like when you're in shape." She smiled, but the magic spell was broken. We soon rolled over to separate sides of the mattress.

As a mediator who has negotiated many settlements, I'm happy to serve as a problem-solver on Paseo Tranquillo. I talk to neighbors respectfully. If there's an issue, I imagine a solution that makes them feel it was their own idea. Emma claims it's charm, but I just detach myself from emotional investment, nod my head, listen, and don't immediately disagree or argue.

Dutch's empty whiskey bottle lay discarded on our lawn the next morning. I went to politely suggest not depositing detritus on a neighbor's property. Perhaps a brief reminder on local recycling policies, as who knew what hellish practices were allowed in Arizona. Wildflowers had been torn from the little beds we'd planted by the curb. Dutch's bouquet?

He busied himself moving long cylindrical packages from the U-Haul into his garage. Over the scant days of his residence, Dutch had already boarded-up the windows facing the street.

"Looks like a bunker now," I joked. "Expecting trouble?"

"Heh. Pretty busy here, Bobster. You got something burning on your mind?"

I displayed the Early Times bottle. "Found this dumped on my grass."

He formed a sneering smile. "Okay, then. Put it in the blue bin for recycling." Dutch returned to transporting the suspicious tubes.

I noticed tall speakers near the garage door. "Setting up a stereo inside?"

"Nope," Dutch shouted. "I'm an outdoors guy. Sound keeps me pumped." He squinted toward me. "You like classic rock?"

I gave a thumb's up before saying, "Remember, neighborhood quiet hours are 10 p.m. to 8 a.m."

"Noted!"

The next afternoon, driving home from mediating at Finkleberg Law Associates, something seemed different. More sky than usual showed as I turned on Paseo Tranquillo. Two trucks sat parked awkwardly between the street and Dutch's driveway. The old fifty-foot Bishop pine tree that grew from his yard but shaded both of our entrances with its widespread branches had been chopped down. Chainsawed sections of the thick trunk lay scattered about; young Latino men tossed pieces into an industrial wood chipper that whined and buzzed. A few elderly neighbors looked on agog.

Amid the noise and wood dust, I found Dutch. "Why? Those pines are the pride of the neighborhood."

He acted cold, indifferent. "Too much shade. Being from Arizona, I crave sunlight, warmth." His mouth curdled. "I'm within my legal rights. Feel free to plant one—on your property."

No reasoning with the man, and the tree had already been felled. Dutch must have noticed me studying his torn-up lawn.

"Doing a Southwestern-style garden," he said. "You Left Coasters should be happy. Much less water use. Irrigation is a pain in my ass." He scowled. "You work for money changers."

"Who told you that?"

"I Bingled you."

"You use...Bing?"

"I done my research."

When Emma returned home from Bikram yoga, her face paled immediately. She soon lay crying on the sofa, inconsolable. "I loved our tree."

"Sweetie, legally it wasn't ours."

"Screw legality. What kind of monster does that?"

I stroked Emma's hair. "Told Dutch about our quiet hours. We'll get through this." That didn't soothe her. "I'll speak to David Garner at tomorrow's neighborhood meeting. We can vote to preserve all historic trees on Paseo Tranquillo."

"Thanks. I'm getting the worst migraine." Emma retreated to the guest room; a signal she desired solitude.

The following days passed without major incident. A shirtless, sweaty Dutch did trim the hedge between our properties, but the alley fencing would prevent him from staring into our downstairs rooms. What went on inside that windowless bunker where a generator hummed and air conditioning ran nonstop?

It took a few mornings to adjust to hearing Quiet Riot, Foreigner, and Ozzy at concert volume around eight a.m., but I soldiered through. Emma instinctively departed for our quieter guest room at dawn. Noise canceling headphones helped. The cumulative result, according to David Garner, my wife, and work associates, was that I'd become edgy and temperamental. Not detached and calm. Just Dutch's influence, or did the daily gym workouts and my new steroid regimen contribute? I had developed muscle tone and slimmed my belly, which made Emma more amorous.

The next week, I sat in a meeting room mediating between two attorneys. After some angry thoughts flashed through my head, I noticed both lawyers looking concerned. Had I been speaking aloud? Sheldon Knopf asked me in my Bluetooth earpiece to step into the hallway.

"Robert..." He placed a hand on my shoulder. Never good in a work situation. "We've witnessed your mood-swings, your outbursts, the nasty comments." He sighed. "Please go home, and forget about Friday."

"Really? But the case?"

"We've got other mediators." Knopf smiled. "Hey, I get it," he whispered. "Every marriage encounters bedroom problems at some point."

"Not. Bedroom. Problems." I breathed in and out so as not to explode.

"Think about counseling, Rob." He waved. "Cheers."

After the gym, I went home. Dutch had positioned a large trampoline at the center of his transformed yard. Dirt ground showed pebbled pathways, with small swaths of buffalo grass, while large cactus trees and a variety of succulents grew. Everything sharp, prickly, spiny. Unwelcoming.

Though the following morning was a day-off, I rose early with Emma. Something about "Cat Scratch Fever" blasting outside didn't encourage sleeping-in. I shaved and brushed my teeth while Emma showered. When she emerged, wrapped in a towel, she wiped the condensation fog off the window.

"Oh my god," she said. "He's jumping on the trampoline—naked." But she kept watching. "Got to say, his shoulders are strong and his ass is firm for what, seventy-two?"

She laughed as I continued brushing. "Oh no, he's turning around." Emma gasped. "I've never seen one that big before."

Really?" I said after spitting out. First this jerkwater jack-off had impressed her with his toned physique and now... For some reason I added, "So you like that?"

"What?" She punched my shoulder. "Jesus, Rob, I meant his sack. He doesn't need a golf bag to carry his clubs." Emma shoved me toward the window. "Enjoy the view while I go vomit downstairs."

I shuddered but couldn't look away. Like a freeway car accident or a grandmother's mustache, it was both repulsive and astonishing.

Apparently, neighbors voiced concerns about children walking home after school, because by Saturday evening when I returned from errands, high bamboo fencing blocked Dutch's front yard. Strolling outside, I lingered at the new gate. David Garner's bulletin had been posted (which I co-authored) stating that Bishop pines and all rare trees were now protected on Paseo Tranquillo.

As if psychic, or employing a hidden camera, Dutch emerged to glower at me. "You been complaining?"

"Not me." I grinned, something in the steroids making me unafraid. "But neighborhood kids don't love seeing scraggly old men with dementia bouncing butt-naked on a trampoline."

Dutch allowed the tiniest curve of a smile. "I like you acting tough. Thought you were a snowflake pussy when we first met." He stared up at my bathroom window. "Saw your wife checking me out. She looked mighty pleased." He tore the bulletin off his gate then threw it at me. "I'm an American. Don't mess with my personal freedoms."

I stood with arms folded. "How you treat your neighbors is how we'll treat you."

"Yeah, whatever." He waved dismissively. "Anyway, you hear about your governor coming to town next week for a fundraiser?"

"Sure. Why are *you* interested?" Here was an Arizona transplant, whose paramilitary clothing and stubbled, raw beef face practically screamed, "January 6th rioter!"

"I kinda like that 'Frisco pretty boy," he replied. "Like to get up close, maybe give him some free advice."

"Okay. I'm heading back to my house on Planet Earth now."

As Emma and I watched *Better Call Saul*, I pondered Dutch's words. He'd been ultra-secretive with those cylinders in his garage. Could they be rifles, tiki torches, Javelin missile shells? What the hell was this backwoods bozo doing in our liberal enclave anyway?

On Sunday afternoon we heard louder than usual trampolining, with the addition of feminine laughter.

Emma peeked out. "How funny. His cleaning lady Yolanda joined him. She worked for the Talbots. I didn't recognize her without her clothes."

"I better see this."

Emma squeezed my forearm. "Remember, body positivity."

I soon retreated, but that spectacle somehow led to us grappling undressed on the upstairs carpeting. An event only marred at its climax when Emma muttered "Justin."

"Who's Justin?"

"Sorry. I read Justin Bieber had temporary paralysis of his face. Poor guy. Guess it was on my mind."

Emma had never been a fan, "a Belieber," and if Justin's career *had* ended, was music and life as we knew it in America irrevocably altered?

Late Tuesday night, I patrolled outdoors using night-vision goggles a friend loaned me. Emma attended her yoga class followed by a wine bar afterwards. Earlier, a barber had cropped my hair close, leaving it spiky on top.

I wore a green cap, camouflage fatigues, and black face paint. Dutch had become my very own Kurtz to vanquish.

I wedged between my alleyway fencing and his bamboo curtain. A security light flashed on, so I crawled until I lay under Dutch's trampoline, invisible. The light switched off. Twenty feet ahead, the sliding garage door hung halfway open, bright illumination within. I could see him hunched over a work table. Dutch attached wires to tubes and metal boxes, then threaded a long string. A fuse. Either rocket shells or explosives. *Meet your new neighbor: the fucking Unabomber!*

I crawled out the same way and rushed into my dark house. When I collided with Emma in the kitchen, she screamed.

"Shhh!" I said.

"For a moment I thought you were Dutch." She flicked on the overheads. "You cut your hair like his. Why the camouflage clothing and black makeup?"

"I had to meet the enemy on his own terms."

"What?" She acted fearful, nervous. "Dressed as...a Proud Boy?"

I rolled my eyes. "He's building weapons in there, maybe bombs. I have to stop him."

Upon calling the Santa Valeria Police Department, a robot asked if it was a 911 emergency or a police complaint? To summon an ambulance or fire engine was a hefty fee, so I chose the latter, leaving a voicemail.

"I just Googled him," Emma said. "Dudley Cragmire died in 2005. Who is that guy?" She held up her iPhone, hand shaking.

"Maybe Dudley's brother, or son. He couldn't buy a place in California with a fake last name."

Emma soon vanished into the guest room; I lay awake for hours, just listening.

No police came that night or the next day. Maybe they assumed it was a crank call. Birds sang, children played, and regular life went on across Paseo Tranquillo.

The following morning at dawn, two vans arrived with men dressed in body armor. They raided his house, searched the garage, dug ditches in the yard. We could hear Dutch protesting, angry and defiant, then whining, pleading. By that point, neighbors had been roused from their slumbers to watch. Clearly, he was resisting, fighting back. "Please don't make us do this, sir," one man said. When a pained howl more animal than human sounded, I knew Dutch had been tased. And again. Emma joined me upstairs in her pajamas to observe. Two big men shoved him into a van. He shook his fist at our window. "I'll destroy you, Bobert!"

Police detectives spoke to me downtown later. "Darren Cragmire had a seizure after being detained," Detective Johnson said. "He's in a coma at Santa Valeria Memorial."

"From the taser?" Neither detective answered me.

"A doctor from Phoenix claimed Cragmire was in ill health, suffered from PTSD since Vietnam." Detective Garcia eyeballed me. "While he possessed an enormous cache of illegal fireworks, we did not find explosive devices or weaponry consistent with domestic terrorism."

"I'm sure I saw—"

"Partially our fault for rushing in, partially yours."

"But his obsession with the Governor of California?"

"We found Cragmire's love letters to Governor Newsom," Johnson said. "Wanted to meet him."

"You can go now," Garcia told me. "We'll be in touch."

During our late pizza dinner, Emma seemed in shock, unable to face me. "I win." I raised my Busch beer in victory. "No more neighbor hassles."

She stared at the table. "I'm leaving you, Rob."

"What?"

"You're wearing a gaiter." Her head slumped. "Kid Rock is playing on your Pandora feed. You've changed into someone like Dutch."

"I did it for us." I chewed on my slice, thinking. "By the way, there's a Justin who works on the library's third floor. Is it him?"

She sighed. "No, it's Justine, my class instructor. We bonded through Bikram yoga."

"Wow."

"Don't know where it's going, but regardless, I can't live here anymore." She went to pack a bag.

Detective Johnson called: "Cragmire's brain activity has ceased. Relatives will decide whether to keep him alive in a vegetative state."

The following weeks felt like a funeral. Mine. No firms requested my mediation. Not Finkleberg Law Associates nor Jensen Legal, not even Merkin & Gherkin. Total silence. I eventually called Sheldon Knopf. "We'll, uh, get back to you, Robert," he said. David Garner visited, wondering aloud if I should sell my place during its market value peak, allowing Paseo Tranquillo to put our stressful neighbors' feud behind it and once again become tranquil.

The house sold for nearly twice what I paid for it. Sitting in my new jeep on the parking strip, I pondered my future. Northern California? Oregon?

Two men in suits exited a black SUV, smiling. They flashed their FBI credentials. "Wanted to thank you," one said. "After extensive investigation, we found parts for a sharpshooter rifle hidden in Darren Cragmire's Suburban, some anti-semitic conspiracy stuff on his hard drive. Cragmire's group believed the Governor had potential as a future presidential candidate. He planned to eliminate him."

"Group? So Dutch wasn't gay but a white extremist?"

"Likely a cover for his real intent. Though many extremists hate the thing they actually are deep inside."

"Member of the Scottsdale Saviors," the other man added. "Reason we came today, is we heard you're unemployed, newly single, and just sold your home. You could work for us."

"I'm a little old for the FBI."

"No, as a deep cover informant who'd join a militia group in Arizona or Nevada. You fit the angry loner profile: clothing, hair, age, race. We expect future incidents at state capitols and voting facilities. Mob violence. You'd contact us beforehand."

It sounded absolutely insane. Was I even myself anymore? Or had Emma been right about me transforming into him? I glanced beyond the driveway at Dutch's abandoned trampoline and back at our dark empty house, then said, "Yeah, sure."

LIFE'S A GAS

He lounged inside the dim palace, his Clarendon Gardens flat that wealth and fame had afforded him. Before noon and already sipping brandy. A mirror lay on a side table with two lines of coke dusted across it. *Leftovers from last night, this morning?* Guitars were strewn about, unplayed, while velvet curtains draped over the windows breathed in the London air. They blocked light and street noise, but the plush furniture and leather accessories did nothing at present to please him. Deep into 1974 and he felt like royalty in exile. Once indomitable, top of the charts, prince of pop, talk of the town, now reduced to gossip column quips on his weight, or the failure of recent singles to crack the top ten charts.

His wife burst into the living room, trembling, distraught. "Marc, I'm leaving."

"Darling, have a drink. You told me the same last week. Last month too." He waved for her to join him on the couch. The television played static as he awaited the BBC to begin broadcast.

June remained standing, her blonde hair tied back severely as she clutched a carry bag. In a short suede jacket and new bell bottoms, she looked on the verge of an overseas journey, or a cross-continent train ride. "I know about Gloria. Thought it was just a fling, but it's been a year."

Marc reached for his glass, failing to nab it. "I *know* you know." Confusion clouded his mind. "I told you."

"So that's all you have to say?"

"You're my wife, I want you to stay. We'll go on as three. It'll be a stone groove, man."

"Not for me," June said. "I'm your fan, your business advisor. You've lost half of your band, and Tony's not going to stick around to produce you—"

"I don't need anyone." He attempted to rise from his slouched position. "I'm the Cosmic Punk." *Why hadn't that expression caught on?* "This is just a lull, an intermission. I've got a whole new musical vision that mixes funk and soul with my sound."

"Marc, you have to clean up. You never used to drink more than a pint of bitters or a glass of champagne. And lose weight."

"I'm not fat!" He felt his stomach surge angrily against his belt. The damn British papers went on about how he'd ballooned from 9 to 11 stone. "I'm retaining water, that's all."

"Right, you're bloated," June said. "You can't connect with the kids or record buyers like that."

"I saw my future in 1970 and it came true," Marc said in his whispery voice. "I saw it again in a dream the other night." He smiled. "I can get it all back, but it has to be in the next three years."

June's mouth twisted downward. "Why, what happens then?"

"I don't know, maybe I become a movie star or a poet. There's so little time. " He scratched his forehead.

She stared at him, one eye twitching slightly. "I came in to let you have it, but there's no point. You're oblivious."

"If you're with me, stay. If you're leaving, leave."

June spun around and rushed out of the living room.

"Wait," Marc said. She couldn't be serious. People threatened things to him then changed their minds. It would blow over, it had to. He needed her common sense. June meant so much to him, if only... He became distracted by the nearby tray of half-eaten food. Munched on a piece of a crumpet, swallowed the yoke of a poached egg, and speared a sausage. It tasted cold and hard. *When had breakfast been served, at dawn?* "Come back," he yelled to no one.

Marc spooled the reels of his super 8 film of *Born to Boogie.* Soon in the darkened room amid the flickering celluloid, there he was fronting the band in all their 1972 glory at Wembley, playing to ten thousand delirious fans. The kids, the groovers, the heads. *Look at thin Marc strut.* He quietly sang along with himself on "Hot Love," his first #1 single. Ringo Starr filmed the concerts. Fans who would have mobbed the drummer during Beatlemania, ignored Ringo at the height of T. Rextasy. Marc reminded himself, that was only two years ago. He could London Bridge the gap between, get back there, where he belonged. Lennon wanted to produce him, Dylan knew his name, he'd offered Hendrix guitar playing advice. Some of those things were even true.

He tried giving Ringo a bell. Maybe they could shoot a Part 2. Some flunky answered. Apparently, Ringo was out drinking with Harry Nilsson. *God, that bender could go on for days.*

His booking agent and confidant Mickey Marmalade entered the living room. After surveying the empty vodka and brandy bottles, the powdered mirror, food remnants, and sputtering film, he said, "You at it already, sire?"

"Where's June?"

Mickey gestured at the window. "Loading her things into the boot of a cab."

"She'll be back." Marc winced. For once not certain, when he'd been cock-sure most of his life. He pointed at the concert film. "Can you get me another show there, man?"

"Wembley?" Mickey's face fell. "Not possible now." He scratched at his chin in thought. "But maybe opening for newer popstars."

"That's jive," Marc said. "I'm the original, the pioneer. They're just following my trail."

Mickey paced the floor. "I can definitely book you at clubs up north, in Denby Dale, Scunthorpe, or West Arsebridge—"

"I don't play rooms, man. Halls, theaters. I'm a superstar." He sighed. "You're sacked."

"You sacked me yesterday."

"And I will again tomorrow," Marc replied. They made eye contact and both cracked up.

"Let me see what I can find." His agent didn't appear certain of anything.

Marc thrust himself off the couch but a dizzy head-rush followed. "I forgot, I booked recording time at the studio. Need to get ready." He knelt down to snort the last lines. "Check outside. A hundred fans camped outside earlier, young girls. I might need to sneak out the back way."

Mickey wore a doubtful expression. "If you say so." When he pulled the purple velvet curtain back from the window, Marc squinted from the sudden blast of daylight. "No one out there," Mickey said. "Just a housewife wheeling a pram."

"Must have moved on to King's Road," Marc replied. "I saw them earlier." He turned toward the food tray, and spying the remaining sausages, he reached.

"Wait till after the session," Mickey advised him. "You always play better hungry."

Marc shuffled across the room toward his wardrobe closet. He dressed up for every recording session like a gig, made each take of a song a performance.

Tony waited at Trident Studios. He expected Marc to be late, and he was. Tony hid his shock at the eventual arrival. In the five months since they'd recorded together, the small, beautiful man had transformed. His face swollen, jowls evident, eyes flashing wide, facial skin slack from alcohol. Tony realized the secret of handsome men: they kept their expressions limited, taut, camera-ready. Rarely ate and smiled only slightly. While Marc was wincing and gurning, pouting and mugging, somehow looking grotesque when that seemed impossible only a year ago.

"Did you bring songs, Marc?"

"I have a notebook full, man." He grinned and gestured. "I'm a superstar, and don't you know it."

Tony laughed. "Yeah, I know."

Jack Green had replaced bassist Steve Currie, but he'd ditched today's session after waiting an hour for the star to show. Tony would have to play bass, maybe keyboards too. "Paul's here and Mickey went out for some crisps." Tony paused. "Let's record whatever today, but I really think we need a break." He fingered his mouth. "A year off, for you to get back in shape, write a bunch of new material. So we can do something better than *Tanx*."

"*Tanx* was epic, man," Marc said. "Don't listen to *Melody Maker* and *NME*. They're jealous because I've had too many chartbusters. They loved me as an underdog, then rained on my hit parade." Marc arranged his feather boas atop his peach satin jacket, and tossed a silk scarf over one shoulder. "You told me yourself that 'Electric Slim,' 'Broken-Hearted Blues,' and 'Highway Knees' were some of my best songs."

"They were strong, Marc." Tony noticed his Brooklyn accent flattening the r sound into "Mahhk." He frowned while drinking from his coffee mug. "But three songs out of thirteen. The rockers were, like you'd done them before, and the soul stuff was..." he wanted to say shrill but couldn't, "not realized. Half-baked."

"Look, man, I'm T. Rex, you're not." Marc stood, head of curls bowed, as if, meanwhile, he was still thinking. "What are you suggesting?"

Tony smoothed his long straight hair down. "We had a magic formula. You did your Chuck Berry thing with hooks, then I added strings and Flo & Eddie on vocals. All of our big hits had that recipe." He knew Marc was superstitious.

"I brought in Gloria and the black chicks to sing backup." Marc rubbed his sweaty face with a hand.

"That's the new direction for *Zinc Alloy*, space-age funk, cosmic soul." When Tony didn't reply, he sank down into a leather studio chair. "But for singles, it's cool to use the old formula. Bring Flo & Eddie to London."

"Well, they want to be paid, Marc, and Paul Fenton and Jack want more than 40 quid a week. I need a percentage too, not just a flat fee."

"Money, money," Marc shouted. "Doesn't anyone care about art except me?" He pulled a flask from his ruffled vest and sipped at it. "Let's Rock."

Tony strapped on a bass in the performance room while Paul sat on the drum stool with a quizzical expression, being new to the circus. Ten minutes later, Mickey Finn drifted in and squatted down to his set of bongos. Habitually a clown, making faces and leaping about in concert, today he seemed bored. His angular handsome features had been a perfect match for Marc—his onstage foil from 1970 through 1973. Now he served as a stark reminder: Marc's face and waistline had thickened, but Mickey remained much the same. The importance of his bongos to their success was questionable, but somehow it had worked. Set T. Rex apart. According to Marc's superstition, to remove his charismatic presence or percussion from the band's mix would surely curse them.

Tony watched the impatient star posing and strutting with his guitar through the control room window. Studio engineers wanted separation at recording sessions so each instrument could be mixed individually, but Marc would have none of that. He demanded they do a couple of takes, all live, together as a band. Tony insisted on rerecording the lead vocals later, since they got lost in the bashing drums. Marc stumbled in on his 4-inch platforms, gave a look to each of the others, then started counting off, "One-two-three-four..."

"Wait," Tony said. "We don't know the chords."

Marc flashed a look of disbelief. "It's in E. Just watch my hands."

They always did, since even if he wrote down the changes, there was no guarantee when he would shift.

Marc got a monstrous tone, all velvety overdrive, from his Les Paul plugged through a Marshall stack. He just grooved on the throbbing E chord as he hammered the 6th note and staggered the beat. What had been a Chuck Berry then a Stones trademark was now his rightful boogie inheritance. He spit out nonsensical phrases about emerald slippers and dark wizards from the forest glades. Right when no one expected it, he lurched to a G chord and sang an almost eastern cascading wail over it.

Tony was excited until Marc just kept repeating the one-chord vamp with an eventual second chord release for ten minutes. Finally, it crashed to a halt.

"Beautiful, man." Marc squatted on the carpeting, his face glowing. Something about the weight gain had made his perspiration copious.

"That's a cool start, like a verse." Tony chose his words carefully. "But it needs a chorus, and maybe a bridge."

"I'm trying to simplify," Marc said, out of breath. "'Get it On' had four chords, so I removed two." He glanced around for affirmation. "Rock is about feeling, not music theory shit."

They stormed through three more shambolic tunes. All groove, without any hooks. Marc shouted out, "Forever boogie," or "I'm the king of boogie," and lastly, "Boogie assassin." He shook his matted corkscrew hair and lunged about, trying to enthuse the others, until the brandy he'd been quaffing sent him toppling ass over platforms into the drum kit. Expensive Neumann microphones suspended on stands crashed to the ground. Nigel Burke, the engineer ran out of the control room in a panic as Tony helped Marc up.

"With your strings on top, Tony, and the singers' soul harmonies, we'll have super-hits."

Tony's smile felt so clenched it almost hurt him. "That's enough for today." He studied his watch. "You have the BBC interview in a half-hour."

"I don't want to do that jive." Marc rubbed his nose. "I never listen to that DJ."

"The benefit gig next week will get coverage everywhere," Tony said. "Your photo in the papers, maybe an interview. Not just a gossip column sighting."

"If you think so..."

"Marc, your manager BP would want you to do this. You can promote *Zinc Alloy & the Spiders of Tomorrow*."

"The Hidden Riders of Tomorrow."

"Please, Marc," Tony pleaded. "And be nice to Andy. You need good press." He put his hands together in prayer. *Would he eventually quit or be fired?*

Marc nodded. "Yeah, okay."

BP Fallon picked up Marc in the Rolls he'd never learned to drive. So many of his songs about cars, yet he remained an eternal passenger. "A quick detour to Fulham Road,"

Marc told him. BP showed a slight knowing smile on his cherubic face. "Better wear a disguise." Marc doffed an outsized top hat.

The car blocked traffic and passersby were stunned by the sight of an outrageously dressed man rushing from a white Rolls Royce into *The Great American Disaster* to soon emerge clutching a burger and fries.

They arrived a few minutes late at BBC Radio London studios. Two female assistants ushered him into the broadcast room where the D.J. sat speaking into a microphone. They delicately placed headphones over Marc's curls and wheeled his chair toward another mic.

"This is Andy Merkin for the Beeb. And look who just dropped in, the former superstar from years past. Does anyone still remember T. Rex?"

Marc restrained his anger; he needed this. "The kids remember," he replied in his softest voice. "The groovers, the sliders, the beautiful people. I play for them... and the gods."

"Marc, you once sold the most pop singles in the UK after The Beatles. What happened? How did you fall?"

"Nobody fell," Marc said. "We had hit after hit. The Beatles were four people, and that level of success became too much for them. I'm just one person, writing, singing, performing, running the record company."

"So you had a nervous breakdown?" Merkin allowed a snort of laughter.

"No, we planned this. To become album artists, not just a hit singles band. I started out in the underground."

"The tube?" Merkin rested his chin in one hand. "Well, you haven't had any major hits, so I guess your plan succeeded."

"You don't have to be so jive with me, man. If you don't dig my sound, what do you like, Alan?"

"It's Andy. At the pub, I listen to Slade and Cliff Richard." He coughed. "You've claimed to have invented glitter rock or glam rock, but never actually played it."

"Yeah, I started it on Top of the Pops in early 1971. But my influences were Elvis Presley, Chuck Berry, and Bob Dylan."

"And Donovan?"

"I think my voice is original, a style I developed."

"Can I play you something?" Merkin asked. He cued a pumping rocker with a vibrating, affected vocal.

Marc shook his head about, tapped his shoes. "That's me. I don't remember exactly. Probably a B-side from an *Electric Warrior* single."

Andy Merkin smiled wide. "No that's The Kinks Ray Davies singing 'King Kong' from 1968. So, did he invent your style?"

"I loved The Kinks, when I was young, but Ray doesn't usually sing that way. For me it's a full-time job, man."

"Okay, here's a more contemporary song." Merkin started "Rock On" by David Essex.

Marc breathed. *Don't let him get a rise out of you. You're a superstar.* "Yeah, David is basically doing me here. The 'Hey kids' lyrics, and the string arrangement is like what Tony Visconti puts on my records. The difference is, no guitar. So it doesn't rock, it throbs." Marc paused. "But I dig the bass player, man."

"What of the other glam rockers, like Roxy Music, or what Bowie's doing on *Diamond Dogs*?"

Marc giggled. "I haven't heard that yet."

"But you're mates, right? He wrote 'The Prettiest Star' for you."

"I played guitar on it."

"Didn't Bowie write 'Lady Stardust' for you?"

"You'd have to ask him." Marc swiveled back and forth on the leather chair. "I dig Mott the Hoople. 'Honaloochie Boogie' and 'Golden Age of Rock and Roll.' I could cover those, man."

"You mentioned in an old interview that you had a book of poetry and three science fiction novels." Andy allowed a long pause. "And yet I've never seen one at a bookshop."

Marc said so many things back when he was high on stardom. "Those books exist, but I'm not in publishing, so I don't know where to find them. There's so little time."

"I see..." Merkin leaned in closer. "Your Tyrannosaurus Rex songs about witches, elves, and unicorns. That was all a load of codswallop, right? You were singing to the acid heads at the end of the sixties."

Marc rose for a moment, saw Merkin appear stunned, then sat back down. "That's cynical, man. There are other realities. I read Tolkien and sang about it, years before Led Zeppelin. This Indian guy is teaching me to leave my physical form, like in *Dr. Strange* comics." He sighed. "Music is escapism, not just marketing and sales." Marc glared at Merkin. "I don't play for the jivers, the bread-heads, the ripoffs."

"So I suppose you think I'm a jiver?"

"I came here to talk about a benefit show for underprivileged children."

"Aren't you just playing that concert to raise your public profile?"

"No, man, I wear bigger platforms to achieve that." Marc pointed at his shoes and grinned. "I'm donating my time for free. Are you giving anything to the charity, Andy, or are you against the kids?"

"I, uh, I am all for the young people," Merkin sputtered.

"You've slagged me this whole interview and you haven't even played one of my songs." Marc threw his hands in the air so staffers could see his frustration.

Merkin froze, distracted, a loud voice spilling from his headphones. His mouth flatlined and eyes went dead. "And let's hear a big hit by T. Rex, 'Children of the Revolution,' a fitting choice for this benefit concert, also featuring Sweet, Suzi Quatro, and the Bay City Rollers." He cleared his throat. "A big thank you to Roly Boly, Marc Bolan, for dropping by today."

When he switched off the mics, Marc lunged. "You bastard. Nobody calls me Roly Boly." He grabbed him by the jacket lapels and shook Merkin until one tore. "You'll always be square. You're the old guard, hair combed over. Grew your sideburns long and wear flares to seem hip."

Suddenly the compact room filled with BBC associates on one side and BP Fallon and Mickey Marmalade on the other, pulling both men apart. Fists swung as curses rang out, a wave of people falling forward then back.

"If I was younger and stronger, I'd teach you a lesson," Merkin shouted. "Sod off now." His voice shook. "You're over. The kids don't care about you or T. Rex anymore. But they'll remember me forever because I'm their Dandy Andy."

It was September of 1977, only weeks from Marc's thirtieth birthday. He felt better, even with the news that Elvis had left the building for good in August. After a long slough, a crawl through muddy trenches, Marc was razor thin and on the way to a comeback. His afternoon TV show, a tight new band, and decent material helped. They had been celebrating at Morton's in London. He was so drunk and tired now though, as his wife drove home fast, very fast at four, or was it five a.m.? Speeding across Putney Bridge, he meant to tell her, "Slow down," but instead said, "Life's a gas." She glanced over then squeezed his hand.

Marc was in a half-world between consciousness and sleep as he rose above their Mini. Astral traveling—just like Dr. Strange. Higher and higher. Below, he could see Knightsbridge, Muswell Hill, Cambridge Heath, and the grumbling tugboats barely moving on the Thames, and then even Ladbroke Grove where he'd lived with June before stardom. He floated through a portal, fusing with the celluloid of his movie *Born to Boogie*. There he sat cross-legged on the carpeted stage strumming "Spaceball Ricochet," much as he had done in the folk duo, Tyrannosaurus Rex, at hippie festivals. All the kids, the heads, and the stone groovers in Wembley were transfixed by his every word. And Marc decided to remain there forever, where he could sing to the thousands flocked around him about the people of the Beltane, the goblins, monsters, and dwarves who thrived amongst the woodland rock, and where a metal guru met a mystic lady under the mambo sun to birth the stars beneath the monolith. Someday, they would ride a white swan up a raw ramp to see their planet queen.

All that fairy nonsense the press had accused him of, actually true, to be fully realized by himself. He didn't need Telegram Sam to tell him that Tony Visconti was his main man, or that he alone could connect James Dean's car to Chuck Berry to Highway 61, because "Bobby's alright!"

Marc laughed.

The impact caused a vibration at the core of the world, one people would feel for years, for decades, even if they didn't sense it then or the next morning, even if they hadn't been born yet, or didn't live in England, or didn't know of him, had never boogied in their lives, or wrote him off as teeny-bopper bubble gum music, trudging through their days serious and stooped, with no glitter descending from their overcast skies. Yet somehow, beneath the surface, under the skin, deep in the coils of their brains, some little perfect morsel of joy—a spark from that brief instant when one is young, beautiful, and truly alive—had been plucked out. And all that lingered was a void, a mysterious sadness for what could not be rightfully explained, much less named.

"He just made me happy and feel less alone," a sixteen-year-old girl said later of him.

Squint toward the firmament above. Make a wish on a star. The science teacher pointed to the domed ceiling of the planetarium in the Royal Observatory. "Most everything came from hydrogen and helium; they expanded and cooled. Over billions of years, gravity caused gas and dust to form galaxies, stars, planets, and maybe us too." She fingered her gray hair. Sixty-three and pondering her retirement.

One of her students asked, "So gas is life?"

The teacher heard a busker somewhere outside the hall strumming a G chord on a folk guitar, like the intro of a song she half-remembered. She imagined a whispery, tremulous voice riding above it and felt a shiver of her youth. A smile spread wide and contagious. "Yes, and life is a gas."

RUBY OF HESPERIA

Brad Walford. Every day he remembered, then put the name on like a pair of pants. Strange that he'd come to stay in Hesperia at age fifty, a transitory town that flashed by when driving on I-15 between Barstow and San Bernardino. The kind he'd thanked his lucky stars he never had to live in. Not a hellish place, but set on California's high country, the Mojave Desert surrounding it. Sparse trees allowed a constant wind to blow hot and dusty much of the year. And when a reprieve came from the blistering heat, winter nights at 3,000 feet elevation turned bitter cold. To Hesperia's immediate north lay Victorville, while beyond city limits to the south, the Cajon Summit plunged for miles and miles toward sea level. A void. The end of the world. A grinding, twisting five-lane highway canyoning downward, testing truck brakes and drivers' concentration.

Brad needed a job that paid in cash, off the books. He started at Belden's Tires.

"You learning the ropes, at your age, Holmes?" Victor asked.

The young guys tightening lugs and patching-up holes regarded Brad with suspicion. They taught him anyway, delighted to have someone else hose down the garage at closing, and roll bald or gashed tires to the dumpster out back—for giant annual tire fires that perfumed the high flatland with burning rubber smoke.

"Are you on the run, boss?" Carlos wondered. They called everyone *boss*, except Jake their actual manager. Jake was sixty going on seventy, staring bug-eyed at the office computer as he sipped coffee spiked with whiskey.

"I worked for a company in a building, wearing a suit," Brad replied. "I got sick of it. Needed a change."

"To this?" Carlos spit. "That's crazy. If any of us had a college degree we'd fight for a job like that." He gazed at Victor and Cesar. "No way. You done some white collar crime shit, embezzlement, counterfeiting." The others laughed, but didn't socialize with Brad beyond work.

Three months into working at Belden's, Jake told Brad, "Let's get a cocktail at Jericho Tavern on Main Street." A dimly lit spot, with neon beer signs, a scarred pool table, and a working payphone. Brad's father had wasted away in dive bars. Waiting rooms where eventually, after last call, came the final call—when an ambulance carted you off.

But now, Brad recognized Jericho as a refuge, an oasis in the desert of modern American culture. A place to dream and lose yourself among past decades. Regulars stared into their drinks, not at their smart phones. And no social scientist had proven one choice was wiser than the other.

"Jim Beam on the rocks, Ruby," Jake said.

Ruby served as afternoon bartender. Brad guessed late-twenties, and she had that pretty but plain thing going on. Female bartenders who worked around admiring and sometimes leering men adopted a similar look, a certain stance. Minimal makeup, hair flat and tied back, no flirtatious smiles or winks. More a taut face set with the grim determination to get through each day without hassle.

"How can someone under thirty be named Ruby?" Brad wondered.

Jake didn't reply. "Let me be honest," he told Brad while nursing his bourbon, "you've got no future in tires." In the background, Starship rattled the old jukebox, building their city on rock and roll.

"I know, I'm ready to move on."

"You can do better." Jake waved to a man drooped forward at the bend of the bar. "Dixon manages Sheet Metal Heaven," he said as Dixon shuffled over.

"Hey, Jake." Dixon lifted his baseball cap—hair matted, forehead sweaty—then pressed it down farther.

"I've got a guy for you," Jake said. "Learns quick. Has outgrown my garage."

Dixon sneezed onto his shirt sleeve and turned to Brad. "You dream of sheet metal?"

"No, not really."

"But you could imagine going to an office, selling it?"

"Yeah, sure. Definitely."

Dixon shook Brad's hand. "See you tomorrow at nine." He raised his drink in toast. "To Ruby, Queen of Hesperia."

Cheers sounded. She stared at the ground while Dixon ambled back to his perch.

Brad finished his draft beer among the jukebox throb, TV football swagger, and grill smoke issuing from a rear kitchen. "Easy as that?"

"Easy as that." Jake set seventy dollars in wages by Brad and loped splay-legged toward Jericho's open door.

Ruby gripped Brad's empty glass. "You done?" At 6 p.m. she vanished out the back way. Her evening replacement, Clete, resembled a top-heavy, former linebacker, who if he fell on you, that would be all she wrote. Game over.

Brad learned more than anyone should ever know about sheet metal. The different brands, their thickness, resistance, weight, appearance. He made it sound sexy over the phone and also chaperoned local customers through the showroom to "feel the steel." Three months in he was bored silly.

"You dreaming about sheet metal yet?" Dixon asked.

"Every night." Brad wasn't lying, but they came more as dull nightmares of a future trapped in limbo.

Their main supplier, Johnny Cortez, said, "Damn, you look good, bro. I mean you were in Aerosmith for what, fifty years, right?"

"That's Brad Whitford, I'm Walford."

Brad rented a room with a mini-kitchen at a former DoubleTree Inn that offered weekly rates for $275. It sat a mere four blocks from Jericho Tavern.

An incident occurred one evening near the 7-Eleven on Main Street, situated between I-15 to the west and Jericho to the east. Deciding to avoid the brethren at the bar, Brad bought Beef Jerky and Hot Pockets. The

Bacardi bottle a holdover from a more cultured past. Afterwards, he hesitated outside. A pink and orange twilight hung over Hesperia, and for a brief time the landscape seemed softer, a desirable part of California, not a dislodged chunk of Arizona or Nevada plunked down on the flight path to L.A.

Brad noticed a teenage girl, all grown-up but likely underage. She loitered in a mini-mall parking lot talking to two men in a Toyota pickup. A Latino with a dark mustache and a white dude with a two-tone haircut and a neck gaiter. Right or wrong, Brad assumed that neck gaiters signaled a pro-assault rifle stance and right-wing extremist beliefs.

The men were laughing while she flirted with them, flexing her budding powers. She wore high-waisted blue jean shorts and a low-cut top. None of Brad's business, so he began heading home until he heard a high-pitched voice. "Let go. I don't want a ride."

The white guy pressed her toward the pickup's cab; the other man held the driver door opened. Both appeared to be mid-thirties, their bare arms showing from muscle shirts.

Brad was no hero, usually indifferent, but she looked his older daughter's age. He had not chosen this street to be the hill he would die on, but as he hustled toward them, everything slowed down. Brad huffing and puffing, the men curious yet unphased, the teenager confused.

"Yo, turn around," the gaiter guy said. "It's none of your business."

Brad continued. "Leave her alone, she's a kid." The girl frowned at what she took for an insult. Cars whizzed by but no one stopped.

"Walk away," the guy said. "Aren't you a little old for this shit? She wants to come with us." His hand still clutched the teen, now pale and confused. He opened a jackknife, revealing a short, blunt blade and frowned. "Give me my baseball bat, Luis."

Luis sat frozen with a quivery smile. "You left it at the park."

Brad broke his Bacardi bottle on a back corner of the truck, the precious rum sloshing into the truck-bed.

"Shit, this fool's nuts." The dude thrust his knife. It tore the shoulder of Brad's flannel shirt but barely scraped his skin. Brad lunged forward and the jagged glass ripped open the guy's top.

The thug laughed for a moment then twitched. "Damn, I'm bleeding." He gripped at his stomach. It was a minor cut, but messy enough, red staining white fabric.

While Luis revved the engine, the guy climbed to the truck's passenger seat. "We're coming back to kill you," he shouted. Followed in a softer tone by, "Hey, wait for us, baby."

As they roared off, Brad photographed their plates with his phone and called the cops. Described the truck. Good thing he didn't expect gratitude.

"You asshole," the young woman said. "I wanted a ride with Kyle, just not Kyle and Luis. You ruined my whole night."

"Those guys are in their thirties and you're what, sixteen, seventeen?"

"I'm eighteen," she insisted, "next December." She pouted. "What right do you have—"

"Where are your parents right now?"

"At home."

"Can you text them to pick you up?"

"They confiscated my phone yesterday. I'm dying without it."

Brad didn't want her to use his phone. He squinted and noticed Ruby smoking a cigarette outside the bar. "You're going to march down to that lady and call your folks on Jericho Tavern's payphone." He handed her three quarters. "Do I have to walk you over myself?"

"Get lost, you creep." She started off, cursing and stamping along. "I hate you!"

Drivers whistled or yelled out to her from cars. The only thing worse than growing old in a spit-bucket town would be enduring it as a teenage girl. He stayed to make sure she didn't cut and run, or hop in another truck. She and Ruby eventually pushed through Jericho's door.

Brad tramped back to his hotel amid the cloud-speckled, blood-honey sky like a knight returning from a battle he wasn't called to, clutching the junk food spoils of his crusade. He stood in the room dark just waiting for brute vibrations of fear and anger to subside within.

The next week, Brad missed Ruby's shifts so Vince served him. The hulking Christian saw no conflict in working at an alcoholics bar, nor in throwing back bourbon shots. On a night with few customers, Vince asked, "Have you allowed our savior Jesus into your life?" He held a magnet.

Brad grinned. "I haven't even allowed him onto my refrigerator."

Jericho regulars included Dr. Bud, Carter, and Phil. Lost older males marooned in a century that gave them the finger every waking morning. Phil sidled up. "Tired of dreaming about sheet metal yet?"

Brad laughed in affirmation.

"Ready to work for at Mesa Construction Rentals?"

"Over by Double Eagle Transportation?"

"Yup." Phil dabbed his forehead with a cocktail napkin. "Heard you're good with walk-in customers." He paused. "We need a people person."

"I like to be paid off the books. Cash preferred."

"You got problems with the IRS, son?"

"No, I'm just old-fashioned."

"Positively prehistoric." Phil frowned and moved his mouth around. "Your cash pay would be less." He offered a salary a bit higher than Sheet Metal Heaven. "And after three, four months I'd have to put you on the books."

"Okay then," Brad replied. He planned to be tucked back into his previous life by then.

The job transition occurred on Monday so he hit Jericho early to avoid encountering Dixon—sore about Brad's quitting without notice. Besides Dr. Bud in the distance, his was the only other ass warming a barstool.

Ruby rushed over. "What you did for that teenager, that was fantastic."

Brad felt stunned. "She told you?"

Ruby smiled and her face lit up like the Christmas tree at Rockefeller Center. "She cursed you every which way in hell, but I got the truth before her parents came. Thought I saw you outside." Ruby slid a tap beer over the bar top. "On the house."

Brad tasted it and winced.

"Sorry it's not cold." Ruby touched his hand. "Power outage earlier."

"I love warm flat beer."

While she laughed, he drank in her features, the cathedral domed forehead, her long slender nose out of a Byzantine fresco.

They spoke throughout that week, and on Friday Ruby said, "Doing anything Saturday? Sometimes I like to go to the city and dance, or dine out."

Did she mean Los Angeles? "City?"

"Barstow."

"Oh. I mean, yeah, sure." He paused. "You do know I'm older than you?"

"Well, obviously." She snorted then lowered her voice. "You're sort of a mystery man." Ruby leaned across the bar until her nose nearly touched his. "I can see that you were once...kind of attractive."

Brad nodded. At fifty, why question the vagaries of a compliment? "You want me to drive?"

"Yes I do." She wrote down her address and hurried off to wait on the regulars.

After their date in Barstow, his inept line dancing, and supper at an Italian restaurant, they began seeing each other. Brad acted aloof at Jericho though, since Ruby mentioned it was frowned on for her to date customers.

A month in, they met for a picnic dinner near the southern edge of Summit Terrace where Joshua trees stood sentry over the Mojave. The wind had mercifully calmed and for once Hesperia didn't feel transitory, the weather something to endure. With red wine in plastic cups, they nestled together watching the color-streaked dusk fade to the west until the moon and stars glowed up high.

Ruby pointed abstractly. "Do you ever wish you could go out there, see what space is like?"

"Why? I have everything I need right here."

While she snuggled closer, Brad experienced a deja vu. Had he said the same thing to Kathy, and to Susan before that? It annoyed him, even if he did mean it now. Brad sensed Ruby shrouded in a private sadness. "Someone as special as you must have been married before. Right?"

"I was." She struggled to form words. "I lost him in Afghanistan."

"Oh, shit. I'm sorry," Brad said. "The Army sent his, uh, back home?"

"No." Her head sank forward. "I guess he's still there, somewhere."

"Missing in action, assumed dead? Terrible." Brad gazed at her then away. "Some relatives are still searching for soldiers lost in Vietnam."

"I'm not looking anymore." Ruby's voice shook. "I turn thirty this month. Have to get on with my life." The mesa had grown colder and she shivered against Brad. They finished the wine bottle in silence. "You've been married too," Ruby finally said, poking his bicep with a finger.

"You Googled me?" Walford wasn't his real last name.

"No. But I'd guess once in your twenties and again in your thirties. Am I close?"

"Practically clairvoyant." He stood. "It's warmer inside my car." On their way he asked, "Where would you go if you could leave Hesperia?"

"Leave, why?"

"Well, if *we* left. Where would you suggest?"

She embraced him, impeding his walking. "You mean move-in together, play house?" The wine had made her sad one moment, giggly the next. "Around Flagstaff," she said. "They have pine-covered mountains and lakes. It never gets hot as here in the summer." She kissed Brad open-mouthed and a thin line of saliva descended from her lower lip. "That's where." Then Ruby stumbled and he helped her back into the car.

Brad took her to Hesperia Lake Park, the zoo, they ate at Flavors of India, and at Golden Gate, the Chinese restaurant. She described their future Arizona cabin on a hill overlooking a valley, enough property for a roving dog. To avoid gossip and banishment, Brad only frequented Jericho after her shifts.

Nonetheless, Dr. Bud ushered him over to a rear booth away from the bar noise. "You've been spending a lot of time with our Ruby." His expression was stern.

"Well, I—"

"You're new here, but she has other men interested in her. They been waiting patient till she got over losing her husband."

Brad inhaled Bud's force-field of ancient aftershave and Right Guard. No one knew what he held a PhD in, but being at least sixty-five with a Biblical beard, people respected him.

"Does Ruby have any choice in this matter?"

Bud scowled. "You don't want to be a claim jumper, cause trouble in a small town."

"No I don't." Brad understood Bud. A man too old, too drunk to ever have a relationship with a Ruby, but a protective, parent-figure who felt they should have a say, in who did or didn't get to date a beloved local bartender. Brad would become that in ten years. It was miraculous Ruby had any interest in him now.

"Thanks for your concern," Brad said. "Not to worry, I won't be in Hesperia forever."

Good." Bud seemed satisfied, then soured. "Don't you go breaking Ruby's heart."

Time soon came to check-in to his old life at Glendale, see if Kathy was amenable to reconciliation. His wife had cheated on him, then Brad cheated on her. But while his office fling ended fast—along with his job—Kathy's affair had taken root and lingered. At that point, she asked him to move out, rent a place nearby. Outraged, Brad abandoned her and his daughters, drove seventy-seven miles away to nowhere and began a new life. He eventually created another identity online, with the pretense of attending Kathy's college, to friend her on social media.

Kathy's most recent Facebook posts hinted she'd split from "Dave" and regretted that relationship choice. Perfect timing to visit Glendale. Sunday night, Brad told Ruby of a job interview in San Bernardino to explain his haircut and new suit.

"You thinking of moving?"

"No, I'd commute." He smiled but Ruby seemed shaken.

"Let's just leave for the mountains now, Brad."

"Really? And not tell them at Jericho?"

Her face took on a tragic cast. "You're right, I guess I'm trapped."

"We'll talk about it soon. I'll be back before you know it."

Brad parked by his former home on Monday morning. Glendale looked the same: ugly buildings sprouting alongside the highway, palm trees and tall pines, the Verdugo Mountains looming. He skirted the house, remembering the sliding glass doors to the back patio were left unlocked by day, due to the neighborhood's safety. He slid one panel open and walked the central hallway.

"Hello, it's Dad. Kathy? It's Bradley." He entered the living room holding flowers.

His seventeen-year-old daughter Olivia stood frozen in the connecting kitchen. "You bastard," she shouted, then threw a coffee mug at him. It shattered on the fireplace mantle. "You ran out on us. You suck." She Frisbeed a bread plate that struck his temple.

"Ow, stop that." Brad rubbed his head. "Where's your mother?"

"She's at work, obviously. To pay for the house, for our schools." Olivia began hurling silverware as he danced and weaved.

Brad noticed his thirteen-year-old daughter teary-eyed in the corner. "Becky," he tried. "Why aren't you at school?"

"We're on vacation, and she goes by Becca now." Olivia held up her iPhone. "I'm calling the police."

"Dial your Mom first."

"She hired a divorce lawyer." Olivia's face became red and sweaty. "Get out!"

Brad darted back onto the patio and toward his car. Neighbors who'd heard the commotion were in their gardens pointing at him as if Frankenstein's monster had run amok. Brad drove to Hesperia, cranked up the hotel room AC, and lay on his bed shivering in the cold dark for the entire afternoon.

On Tuesday, Brad returned to work after his "day off." As he donned a hard hat to patrol the vehicle rental yard, Phil grumbled past him. "Everything okay?" Brad asked.

"I need you official, on the books. State's coming down on me."

Instead of *yes*, Brad said, "I understand."

Plan A had failed, so time for Plan B. However, when Ruby didn't reply to his texts on Tuesday or Wednesday, Brad dropped by Jericho Tavern on Thursday. "Where's Ruby?"

"She took three days off, was feeling sick." Clete yanked Brad halfway over the bar. "You didn't knock her up, did you?"

Brad broke free. "No!"

"Management says you're eighty-sixed." Clete gestured toward the door. Behind him, Dr. Bud, Dixon, and other regulars glowered at Brad as if he'd caused Ruby's absence.

Late Friday at Mesa Rentals, Brad confided his plan to his pal Nestor. A two-man job.

"You're nuts," Nestor said. "But throw me a twenty and I'm in."

Brad went to his hotel room, changed into the Glendale suit, wrapped a dozen roses he'd bought earlier, and found the zirconium ring. It was ridiculous, a place-holder. Marriage impossible until a divorce from Kathy could be finalized, though an open-ended engagement sounded perfect. Caught himself whistling. His father did that, but never him.

Brad met Nestor at the closed vehicle rental lot while the sun died to the west. They keyed-up a knuckle boom lift and drove the truck north to Ruby's apartment complex.

She lived on the third floor, so in the parking lot, Brad climbed into the lift bucket and Nestor worked the levers to extend the crane on the truck bed upward. How could Ruby not laugh, not melt at this eccentric proposal?

The beeping and ratcheting caused neighbors to gaze startled from their apartments, but seeing Brad in a suit, hair slicked back, and clutching a dozen roses somehow stopped them from calling the cops. He knocked on her darkened window, squinting. Maybe Ruby *was* sick and sleeping-in. No response. Brad pried the swing-away window open then clambered inside.

Deserted. A few discarded pieces of furniture haunted the rooms. Brad switched on an overhead light; a handwritten note lay atop the living room coffee table.

Brad, or whoever you are, maybe you returned to where you came from. If you're reading this, I've left. I lost my husband in Afghanistan, but he didn't die. Just dead to me after five years. He came back, so I'm meeting him near San Diego. Don't come looking for me because Ruby was my grandmother's name. The Sheryl Crow tune on Jericho's jukebox, "You're My Favorite Mistake." That was our song. Take care, Love - "Ruby"

Brad's shoulders trembled, his eyes watering—realization brutal. Ruby had been Plan A all along, but he'd been her Plan B. Nestor's voice called him from outside. He crumpled the note, maneuvered into the bucket, and descended. More tenants stared agog.

"You look terrible, half-dead," Nestor said inside the truck's cab. "She say no?"

"Already gone." Brad tossed the flowers onto the pavement.

He slept and drank the weekend away in his hotel room. At Mesa Rentals on Monday, Nestor told Brad that Phil had left a message. "Boss said this was your last day."

"Really?"

"Something about you not being legit, not giving a real social security number."

"Right..."

Late afternoon, Nestor came to Brad's desk in a panic. "Two dudes are waiting in the lot and one's got a baseball bat. Said they spent a night in jail 'cause of you. They look like tweakers, bro."

Karma. The guys he'd tussled with. "No problem." Brad put on a hard hat and took the rear office door to a chained-off section of the rental lot, inaccessible to customers. His college roommate, Billy-Dog, a twenty-three-year-old freshman, had recommended making your final day on the job memorable, so they'd never forget you. Brad turned the ignition on an earth grader and rumbled it along. With its odd shape and massive snout it seemed like a cubist metallic dinosaur. He snapped the lot chain with ease then aimed for the familiar parked Toyota pickup. Brad rammed the back bed hard and its tailgate caved-in.

The gaiter guy shouted something beneath the churning engine noise. He thwacked the earth grader with his baseball bat until the bat snapped in two.

Brad forced the pickup truck forward, wedging it into the metal dumpster by the security fence with a satisfying demolition derby steel crunch and windshield crackle. Then he drove out toward the highway.

His father had counseled him: "Find that one true thing in life, son."

"But what if I don't recognize it when I do?"

"Likely won't," his father said. "Most of us only see it in the rear-view-mirror after it's gone."

Kathy had called him a wrecking ball, forever leaving destruction in his wake. Now Brad felt like an impacted building, gutted and hollowed-out, his foundation structurally unsound. He soldiered on regardless. Above and ahead to the north, beyond a few scudding clouds, the blue sky stretched forever—ceiling unlimited. Traffic boiled up behind his slow-moving vehicle on I-15 and sirens began wailing. If he ever got out of this alive, a cabin in the mountains near Flagstaff sounded pretty damn good. Hell, Hesperia would never forget Brad Walford.

Somewhere outside San Diego, a still young woman woke in a motel bed next to the snoring crewcut stranger who was her husband. She could take this ride, try to make it work, and if not, move on. Maybe to Hawaii. She thought of her dead Aunt Debbie. That was as good a name to wear as any.

BIG SUR IMPOSSIBLE

How do you even know when you're there—at the epicenter? A thought as you drive north from Cambria on California Highway 1 past San Simeon. It's not really a town to arrive at, more of a region, a state of mind. We can get all *National Geographic* and speak of a rugged land mass where the Santa Lucia mountains slide right down to the ocean. Besides the sudden cessation of palm trees, that's maybe the only clue it's coming. You round grassy meadows beyond the elephant seal strewn beaches, still near enough to the sea to smell its raw funk. Then you take the first of many hairpin curves, down through a riverbed before rising up into jagged hills of rock and yellow-brown dirt. Sense the altitude, the sky through cypress trees. Yes, it's beginning...

From the 1990s to now, I've driven Big Sur from the south, from the north, hiked the mountains and coastal trails, stayed in its motels, once at Ventana—long ago— and at a monastery on a ridge. I even lived there, as close to the middle of a vaporous place as one can be, yet still can't quite fathom it.

Roll into Ragged Point. Is this inn/restaurant/gift shop propped on a wide mount overlooking the water Big Sur? No, more the southern boundary of the Big Sur Coastline: a ninety mile span that most don't consider before driving it. Ninety minutes? More like two hours, if you're lucky enough not to be trapped behind a caravan of Winnebagos and RVs sputtering along. The first thirty miles seem amazing, fantastic, primordial, magic. But doing the whole journey in one shot is a test of focus, of braking and accelerating, of steering through extreme turns, all the time watching out for oncoming drivers drifting across the yellow lines on a slim two-lane highway carved through a wild terrain not quite ready to sacrifice that wildness.

The worst hairpins appear early on. Feel relief when you reach Gorda, a flyspeck town famed for the pale, enormous Gorda Rock, and also, the highest gas prices on the entire California Coast. Many drivers and families are ready to pause at their deli, maybe stay at the hotel, or brave the restaurant. I say "brave" because instead of hearty grills serving pub fare, local restaurants tend to be gourmet spots with French chefs and astronomical prices. You're not an eighties rocker or a Hollywood star traveling with an entourage? Sorry... The best deals are $10 sandwiches incubating behind frosted glass in delicatessen refrigerator units.

Visitors come to Big Sur for the postcard views, the contrast from whatever clustered city or town they inhabit. It truly seems like a lost paradise, at least for a weekend in good weather. Why do artists and seekers come? Why have I returned over and over, after forsaking it and moving away, after forgetting it for years during wildfires and highway slides? The human desire to make sense of it, to grasp it, possess it, take a little piece home with you to burn eternal. And that's why I try again—failure guaranteed. You can't put your arms around Big Sur and give it a bro hug, can't somehow insert yourself and become one with nature. Too fucking large. And just when everything finally seems clear enough to define it, to impose logic, the fog sweeps in to obscure the borders between land, sky, and sea.

Beyond Gorda comes a two-mile strip of straight, level highway. Tourists remain slow and cautious; they can't trust the 55 speed limit after fighting the road's hazards for a half-hour. I accelerate up to eighty, maybe ninety, to pass the sluggish vans ahead. A dizzying, joyous rush. Only once in many trips did I race by a hidden patrol car. Claimed he was doing me a favor, marking me under 75 mph, instead of the double-charge for above. Still a hefty ticket. Now I know where to slow down, near the ruins of Pacific Valley Station. Hear the scree-scree-scree! of seagulls circling overhead while foamed waves detonate against immense rocks. Getting closer now.

I stop at Lucia, a vague hint of a town made up of a hotel with a gift shop and gourmet restaurant, but only the hotel is still open after a 2021 fire. Troubling, as I will be staying nearby at a retreat room where the Benedictine Monks live, mountain high above the coast. Their provided dinner is limited to a light salad, a questionable soup, and peanut butter and jelly sandwiches. Options? Drive twenty minutes back to Gorda in darkness or thirty gut-twisting minutes north to Big Sur proper. No, it's not a village, but a flash of restaurants, art galleries, and hotels sprinkled along both sides of the route.

The monks have retreated to solitude; visitors are asked to refrain from talking. So there is beatific calm up above, a demigod sensation while you watch the procession of tiny cars far below. Cell phones won't work, nor is there WiFi. Can we exist in a 1999 reality or have we become too spoiled? The only options at the hermitage are vigorous walks and reading books, yet these restraints eventually reveal a world we have trampled over. Of following a single pursuit rather than multitasking, of watching time unfold through nature and the advance then retreat of light. I can't stay aloft for long. Though burning to escape the speaker-phone volume of the California masses, extended isolation can be daunting. Acoustic guitar strapped on, I whisper-sing far from neighboring ears, barely fingering the strings. The silence is so overwhelming, it feels almost rude to strum chords and bellow into the void.

North of Lucia, comes the forbidding sign for Esalen Institute: *By Reservation Only*. No drop-in visitors. The once expensive bohemian center—to realign your chakras—has become even more exclusive, more pricey. Where Bay Area CEOs can microdose or take ayahuasca as they soak in hot tubs while downsizing 25% of their staff remotely. Drum circle freakouts for trust fund influencers seeking meaning within their artificial sweetener lives. Here, even the eucalyptus groves smell expensive. When you can sense wealth behind electric keypad gates, the high fencing walls skirting the highway, you are passing the millionaires' bohemia.

Spirituality and New Age culture has deep roots on the Big Sur Coast. Throw a lilac in any direction and you'll hit a yoga instructor or a massage therapist. But where there is light, darkness exists too. Rumors of witchcraft and cults hidden beyond the ridgeline. In reality, more a flirtation with Wiccan practices: casting spells, exacting revenge on the soulmate who souled you out.

Various sober residents have spoken of the Dark Watchers, who appear in shadowed forests and between giant granite outcroppings. They are described as either "little people" or tall, thin wraiths. Stories persist of a 19th century sea captain who shipwrecked his crew off the rocky shore. Are those sea lions howling at night or the cries of phantom sailors? Some say a female ghost haunts Palo Colorado Canyon; others insist the recreational drugs are very strong in that redwood-shrouded cleft. It is common to hear of landlords burning sage to clear their homes of bad spirits. Are they cleansing demons and witches, or the monsters within us that can be unleashed by living alone for extended periods, living in a chaos without clear rules, clear logic?

My former landlady for a tiny redwood cabin, interviewed contractors in 2008 to get an estimate on a staircase repair. When she turned them away, I asked if the estimate was too high?

"No," she said. "They had ghosts. I could see them in their faces and I won't hire haunted people."

It was later explained that she had glimpsed traces of their past as criminals, of jail-time, of drug use. Paranoia, superstition? Longtime Big Sur residents have their own survival methods, divining rods. Some of it sounds like pure hokum, yet they have endured—in a place difficult to endure in. Drive by and all you see is beauty, serenity, the perfect getaway. To actually live there means dealing with extreme winds and cold, summer heat and wildfires, rainstorms and mudslides. To be one with nature means your neighbors are not only raccoons and skunks, but rattlesnakes, scorpions, bobcats, and mountain lions. All tangible things though. It's the remoteness, the lack of a true center that can slowly warp the solitary mind.

John, *the skunk whisperer*, told me tourists got the best Big Sur experience. "They don't have power outages while their redwood cabin is leaking in a storm." The lanky, gray-haired man relocated skunks from fouling residents' nightly air off to distant parklands.

Approaching Julia Pfeiffer Burns State Park, the route rises high and turns come fast. Views along twenty miles of coastline are staggering—*Look, don't look*—both beautiful and heartbreaking. Epic Greek tragedy shit. The contrast of the timelessness of nature and our own brief lives is crushing. *Concentrate.* Have you heard of the Highway 1 Club? Not something to seek membership in. A designation for people who have driven off the road, off the cliff, and somehow survived. I attended traffic school after my 2009 Big Sur speeding ticket and a 1980s safety film played of a man discussing how he reached for a cassette on his car's floor and when he looked up, was plummeting downward. The camera focused on his unscathed face before panning back to show him in a full body cast. The audience laughed and gasped.

The descendants of the original ranchers who settled the "Big South" are a close-knit bunch who want nothing to do with newcomers or tourists. The rich rockstars and Hollywood denizens own impressive homes they rarely visit, perhaps Thanksgiving this year and Memorial Day next year. Mentions are made of Eric Clapton or Peter

Gabriel, but not of seeing them, just their property. Those without fortunes, the post-collegiate youth, seek to play badass at the farthest reach of the once wild west. They work at bars and restaurants, often pooling together to live four to a cabin up a remote forested canyon.

I found it difficult to connect to strangers while living a quarter-mile from Nepenthe. The artists and writers nearby created in solitude, and were not gregarious by nature. Some locals acted friendly, at least on the surface. *What do you do?* is a loaded question. A reticence to dig too deep. There are forest rangers, carpenters, bartenders, and body workers, but also a whispery world of weed, methamphetamine, and guns. A secret economy. This is not to say residents act unneighborly. In a fast-spreading wildfire, Big Sur locals are heroic in their dedication to help others. During normal times, self-sufficiency is key, is expected. Rental housing remains rare and always expensive. Van life, camper life are a reality. Keep moving. You can't stay overnight at tourist turn-outs.

I finally reach the heart of this vague place, roughly thirty miles south of Carmel. I'm visiting Henry Miller Library for an author's book event. Again and again I've done this. I have been the author; I have been the audience. Parking was packed tight out on Highway 1 and yet few lingered inside the grounds. Cell reception is terrible under redwoods and WiFi access only sprouts in select spots, leading to parked cars filled with Internet desperadoes. So we attend ghost events from a fading culture of books, of readings, of live bands, while the highway traffic remains jammed. "Tell us about your name," library director Magnus asks the author, not for a crowd on the lawn like back in 2014, but for microphones and a podcast. He continues: "Something has happened with publishing…"

The traveling masses scout for a wide level spot, somewhere stable with an Ambrosia Burger reward, and a coastline view for an Instagram-worthy photo. Nepenthe becomes their small city on weekends, parking impossible, while downhill nearby, poets read to spirits, musicians play to impatient audiences wandering in and out of performances. How do you eliminate artists? Name their town an art colony.

What about the original hipsters, beatniks, and iconoclasts? Allen Ginsberg witnessed his generation's best minds "destroyed by madness, starving hysterical naked." And you might see your neighbors emerge from their redwood homes in a similar manner. Many tried to capture the local essence. Jack Kerouac came south to escape the unending drinks and parties accorded to him in San Francisco and he described the waves crashing against mammoth offshore rocks in poetry. But Big Sur didn't soothe him, instead supplying a different form of insanity. Hunter S. Thompson hunted feral pigs in the hills and valleys during the early 1960s, yet he couldn't last long either. Henry Miller grasped the folly of artists believing Big Sur would enhance their creativity, seeing how the vastness of nature overwhelmed them. Mere specks in a primal universe where the elements take charge. Thought you were going to write a novel? No, you built a fence after the previous one rotted from the rains and tumbled down in a mud slide. Miller committed to an austere life high on Partington Ridge. Even he, one of its kings, had to eventually leave for Los Angeles.

So it's useless to write love letters, to declare your undying affection. Big Sur is not hateful, just indifferent. It has seen us come and go for eons. Our lifespans less than an instant in its cosmic consciousness. Big Sur is the crust of the Earth exposed, the jagged western edge of a continent maintaining structural dignity against a relentless ocean. The beauty you see for an hour, a day, a weekend, is one frozen image in the constant chaos dance of creation and destruction. Store everything beautiful inside and travel on. Any paradise that makes you immediately wish to move to it and live there, is often the one to be most suspicious of.

I came to Big Sur hoping to make connections, wanting to achieve things. Ego jive. I left like any tourist, holding only the aching wonder of the landscape. I'll try it again as soon as I forget all of this. And again again after I forget all of that.

DISHEVEL ME

At age forty-four, Susan Campbell shouldn't have been living in a hallway called a one-bedroom apartment on East 62nd Street in Manhattan. Though the dank, noisy flat cost $3,200 a month, her rental agent insisted, "It's a steal." Originally a long, slender studio apartment, the landlord had separated the back third with a wall into a cramped bedroom overlooking an air shaft. From outside the bedroom, the corridor expanded slightly to a kitchen area that merged with the suggestion of a living room.

Susan returned to the postgraduate existence of her early twenties when her marriage to Bill Eaton in the Hudson Valley crumbled earlier in 2019.

After trudging downstairs from her fifth floor walk-up, Susan launched out of the vestibule into the perpetual chaos of city life. Uptown traffic unloaded from the 59th Street Bridge onto the slim exit avenue crossing just west of her building, then it veered east toward First Avenue. Toward her. The constant thrum of pent-up male energy rolling in at night to eat, drink, smoke, snort, fuck, or fight, before retreating in the bleak hours before dawn to whatever boroughs it had emanated from. Rap and reggaeton and classic rock and heavy metal and techno and dance pop rumbled from vibrating cars.

"Hey, uptown girl," a man in a silver Camaro yelled.

Susan didn't show any acknowledgment.

"Want to go downtown?" The light changed and a dissonant fanfare of car horns boiled up from behind. He screeched away.

Pedestrians spoke foreign languages into their phones, chiding, pleading, demanding.

Susan made a quick threat assessment. Thai food delivery guy on his bike leaning against a gate while he texted. *Harmless.* Bald man talking to a half-eaten sandwich pressed to his ear like a phone. *Sketchy.* Black dude, fiftyish, wearing a flap cap, attempting to hand out cards on the corner. "What's your first name, baby?" he asked passing women. "Because I know your last name's gonna be mine." *Preposterous.*

Susan wrapped a wool scarf shawl-like around her head and hustled eastward to pick-up necessities. Catching her reflection in a shop window, she winced. *Why can't I be exotic?* Susan longed to be as strangely beautiful as the artsy girls at the Guggenheim Museum on Saturday evenings. Instead, she possessed the healthy complexion and sandy brown hair of ladies who rode in polo matches, played tennis and golf. Women who proudly wore visors and lunched at country clubs.

From outside, nothing appeared remarkable about Place Market on First Avenue. The green awning draped with clear plastic sheets created an artificial foyer to display fruits and vegetables in wooden crates, then a welter of wildly overpriced basic goods sat inside a narrow store. The only thing unusual about it was the night manager working the counter. To find a handsome guy with alluring stubble employed in a dingy food mart in Manhattan seemed freakish.

Whenever Susan visited, Pete—as she gleaned from his use of the third person—addressed her. "Looking good," he'd say, or, "Pete's day just improved," before depositing her purchases in a paper bag. His flirtation never went beyond compliments and an arch smile, so Susan saw no reason to avoid Place Market. Especially on wintry November nights.

Certainly Susan liked attractive men, but the onset of middle-age brought her a new clarity. Why would a thirtyish man work at a generic market? He must earn minimum wage, affording him a squalid flat out in the Bronx or Far Rockaway. This belief kept Susan from flirting back, as she would have in her post-collegiate days—when money or where one lived didn't matter. Only the hunger for connection did, for the heat of another body to stave off the loneliness of such a crowded yet impersonal city.

Tonight, Pete rang her up and shivered. "How's Pete going to stay warm in here alone?"

Susan's mouth tightened. "Hot tea, coffee?"

"But I'm chilly all over." His eyes widened.

"Maybe try Vicks VapoRub." She clutched her bag and departed.

Crossing First Avenue, Susan considered tucking into some chicken soup and a tuna sandwich at the Ritz Diner, but continued homeward. When the only leftover Greek diner of the neighborhood treated her like a regular, the same as the ancient Jewish men and blowzy Russian women who measured out their solitary days through breakfast, lunch, and dinners served inside, that was a bad sign.

Once she had gasped her way back up to the fifth floor, Judith texted. Susan ignored it. Then she called. "Mom, I just got in."

"You know I worry about your neighborhood, Susie."

"It's the Upper East Side."

"Not really," Judith said. "But speaking of, I ran into Preston Pompay yesterday. He's divorced now too."

"Yes, I heard." Preston was one of those annoying men that bounded from triumph to triumph, living off inherited millions from his grandfather's invention of the flush lever on a toilet. Even his summer divorce had been a courteous affair. Recent photos on society pages showed the divided couple smiling, arm-in-arm, declaring a lifelong friendship of mutual respect.

Sickening.

"Anyway," Judith continued. "Preston goes to the Paradigm Sports Club on 61st Street, so I thought you—"

"That's why you're calling?" There was something embarrassing, and moreover pathetic, about being set-up with a former high school boyfriend at her age.

"I promised you'd join him for lunch tomorrow," Judith said. "Look, he may not be interested, but still, Preston has single male friends." She paused. "I won't let you wither away like that Dickens woman, just because you failed in your marriage."

"Miss Havisham?" Susan said.

"Will you meet him?"

"Just this once." Susan flashed to her collegiate past. "Mom, do you remember Dante? He had such a way with words."

"The poet? It's financially irresponsible to get involved with a writer." Judith sighed. "How's your job search going? Maybe something more permanent?"

"Got to go. Food's burning. Love you." Susan pressed her iPhone's red button. She gazed at the *Cosmopolitan* cover atop the magazine stack on the coffee table mocking her.

Special Issue*. Your Forties: Best. Sex. Ever; Make the Most of Your Sexual Peak; Cougar Confessions; 28 Hot Sex Tricks; Home Alone—How to Blow Your Own Mind.*

Standing on the corner, Susan shielded her eyes and stared upward. The Paradigm Sports Club rose seven floors in gleaming opulence. Cardio rooms, basketball, a swimming pool, a boxing ring, Pilates, and Zumba. Susan considered joining before learning of the $350 monthly membership dues, along with an $900 enrollment fee.

They met in the lunch area, where goat's milk smoothies, heated kale salad, and other healthful, noxious-tasting concoctions were served. Preston appeared perpetually tanned. He had the geometric, slightly receding hairline of actors in black and white movies. It said: Yes, I'm getting older, but the bulk of my follicles are planted in rich soil and will remain firm as they slowly gray in a polite, socially-acceptable fashion.

"Just finished my squash match." Preston hugged her. "Susan, you look amazing," he said, pulling back, "for your age."

"We're the same age," Susan replied. "Actually, you're a year older."

"Yes, funny that men get more distinguished in their forties..." His voice trailed off. A ping sounded. "Excuse me, it's my wealth manager."

What a dick. Wonder who he voted for?

"Damn, the market is bad today." Preston set his phone down, frowning. "Anyway, we're both single and I had a mutually beneficial proposal to run by you." His forehead showed a glaze of athletic perspiration, but even his musky body odor smelled expensive, exclusive.

Was Preston Pompay going to propose marriage? And treat it with the cold calculation of a financial merger?

"I thought we could become an item." His nostrils dilated. "I need someone to attend functions with. The opera, ballet, art openings, sporting events." He stroked the raised golden crest on his blazer's breast pocket as if it was a nipple.

Reality blurred for Susan among the conversations of twenty and thirty-somethings at neighboring tables. All those healthy specimens who endured heroic workouts and sweated bottled vitamin water and ate nutritious meals then excreted organic solid waste.

"You're asking me out?"

Preston glanced up from texting. "You'd be my companion, but our relationship would remain as is. My interests are, somewhat different."

For a moment, Susan imagined him trussed-up in a Brooklyn S&M dungeon.

"So you need a beard?"

"Not at all," Preston insisted. "Anyway, it would be lucrative, and Judith mentioned your financial situation."

Susan didn't even want to split the exorbitant check for her eggplant on gluten-free zucchini bread sandwich, so she said, "This is all very sudden. Can I think about it?"

He smiled. "Of course." He signaled the waiter. "Charge it to Pompay."

Back at home, Susan draped herself in a blanket to watch the TCM network. Middle-aged men and women looked dashing and mature in the old films, dressed to the nines while they smoked and drank at endless parties, then traded witty banter in a precise, clipped manner.

Emma and Christina, former co-workers, invited Susan over to a Williamsburg folk festival. She didn't text back. Both pushing forty, they still thought happiness existed just one borough, one aging hipster away.

Sometime after dinner, a knock sounded. Susan froze. Number one rule in Manhattan: never answer your door. Two bolt locks had been installed for a reason. It could be a food delivery guy; they usually just slid menus under nearby doors. Susan had wedged an area rug to block such maneuvers.

An hour later, her annoying friend Pam texted. *I dropped by, lights were on, but no answer. Hope I didn't interrupt anything. Pop by tomorrow, I have a job idea.*

In the morning, Susan visited Pam's cubicle in the Manhattan Temp Agency on 54th Street and Lexington. "I missed you yesterday," Pam said. She had frosted blonde hair and a prominent jaw, while her eyes looked weird, like they had been done, or needed to be done, or had been done badly. Who knew? After forty, everyone in New York became an impostor of their own identity.

"How did you get into my building?"

Pam ignored her. "I went searching for bottled water in your hood. Have you seen the hottie at Place Market?"

"Yes," Susan said, "but he's thirty, if that."

Pam formed claws with her hands. "We're cougars; we pounce." She growled. "Why does he work there? Did he lose a bet?" Pam fanned herself with a notepad. "He makes disheveled look so hot." She stared at Susan. "Has he asked you out? His name is Pete, right?"

"Not sure," Susan lied. "I don't really date younger men with no money anymore."

"Don't waste your prime," Pam whispered, then snorted. "At our age, we have to act before it's all hot flashes. Make a move. Worst case scenario, you shop elsewhere."

Susan fumed over her saying "at our age." Pam was at least ten years older. She exhaled and focused. "You texted me about a job?"

"I saw your ex last week," Pam continued, oblivious. "God knows why, but Bill's still crazy about you." She glossed her lips. "Can't you just forgive him? It's not like he cheated or went to a hooker. I mean, do you want to be alone, schlepping up five flights to a musty apartment when you're fifty? Or in you're sixties, with a heart condition?"

"Let's have drinks sometime if you wish to discuss my personal life." *Which would be never, ever.*

Pam wheeled her swivel chair back. "There's a wealthy man visiting Manhattan. Vasily Kozlov. He needs a woman within fifteen years of his age to accompany him to a benefit party in the Hamptons."

"A Russian? That feels weird after what's been going on."

"No, he's Estonian. Absolutely detests Putin."

"I'd be his escort?"

"Not what you're thinking," Pam said. "Haven't you heard about Plus One, the platonic companion service?" Pam typed on her keyboard and turned the screen toward Susan, then scrolled down.

Elderly male seeking female, sixty to seventy, for weekend dinners at 14th Street coffee shop. $25 per hour, plus food.

Married woman needs male to go clubbing and dance. Must be gay. $50 an hour.

Brooklyn dude looking for a bro to drink IPA after work. $15 an hour or two beers.

"Wow," Susan said.

"It's part of the gig economy." Pam tapped her nails against the desk. "A program alerts me to big spenders' posts. I already accepted Vasily's request, just need to find someone qualified." She studied Susan. "It's totally safe, Vasily has a five star rating. His mistress is unsuitable for social functions. He wants someone classy to make him look respectable and you have the hard-won features of a first wife." Pam paused. "$500 for six hours work, plus tip. If it goes well, I can get you weekly gigs. You're the perfect sexless date."

Susan swallowed her anger before it vomited out of her. She needed money to make next month's rent. "Don't you have anything in graphic design or editing?"

The neighboring cubicles all fell silent. Pam gave Susan an exasperated look. "You could always sublet your apartment on Airbnb."

"But where would I stay?"

"Oh, right, you're single," Pam said, as if that was a rare, incurable disease. "With your mother in Mystic?"

Connecticut? A living museum where everyone was fossilized and white, and nothing ever happened after nine p.m. Susan took a deep breath. "What should I wear?"

"Try to look country club sexy, not downtown skanky."

Susan trekked the eleven blocks home in a daze. Over the course of their ten-year-marriage, she had grown bored of Bill, then annoyed as he blew through his savings and inheritance by betting on sports, by losing in Atlantic City. The more he gambled and traveled, the less she desired him when he was around. The miscarriage didn't help intimacy either. They had sex on occasion, but unlike their first years, she did everything to wrap up the whole event in ten minutes max, so she could get back to binge-watching a Netflix series. At some point, she wouldn't touch it anymore. Except on Bill's birthdays, maybe Christmas, and when she was really, really drunk. There didn't seem any point, as it no longer brought Susan pleasure to give him pleasure.

Bill did cardio at the Hudson Athletic Club, then followed the workouts with a sports massage from Rutger, a German glandular specimen. Whatever kept Bill out of the house and exhausted was fine with Susan.

One Saturday evening she needed Bill. Her debit card had been temporarily frozen and the bank was closed. When Susan couldn't find Bill downstairs in the club, she climbed to the third-floor massage rooms. The hallway lay dark and silent, so she tried the doors. *Empty, empty, empty, holy shit!* Inside the fourth room, Susan discovered her husband reclining across a massage table while a tough Slavic woman with a meaty face stroked him beneath his towel. A happy ending? Yes, and in a sports club from a lady who could have been a shotput thrower on the Soviet Olympic team.

"That's it," Susan had shouted. "We're done." Then she slammed the door on their marriage.

In retrospect, six months after the divorce, it all seemed absurd. Susan wouldn't touch her husband, and yet she felt humiliated and betrayed when a foreign woman—who had no desire to steal Bill away—performed the same service to make a little extra, non-taxable income. The complications of a modern relationship had rocketed beyond Susan's comprehension. Emotionally, she was in the right, but logically, among the roiling sea of flawed marriages, theirs had hardly been the most compromised.

Susan woke from an afternoon nap with a throbbing migraine, the noise of a ratcheting jackhammer pounding outside. Ibuprofen wouldn't do. She needed Excedrin Migraine, and not some puny child's dose, but three caplets—at least. She made herself presentable before dashing to Place Market in the fading dusky light.

After Pete dealt with other customers, he gave Susan his full attention.

"Hey, gorgeous." He gazed toward the street. "You live nearby?"

Susan was not in a good mood, but Pete looked so cute with his hair cut short in the back while hanging boyish in the front, she said, "That's a personal question."

He flexed a lazy smile. "Pete's taking a scientific poll. Do you come here for convenience, or travel farther to this specific market?"

She smirked and handed him a ten. "Convenience."

"So you do live in the neighborhood." Pete scratched his stubble and pulled change from the register. "Well, if you ever need someone to walk you home at night, for safety."

"That might..." Susan stopped herself. *What did she really know about Pete?* "This is Lenox Hill, not the South Bronx," she said. "But thanks."

He outstretched his hands, palms up. "I don't even know your name."

"You'll have to guess." Susan gripped her Excedrin and pushed through the glass door. In which she could see Pete's reflection checking her out. She felt annoyance, mixed with a perverse satisfaction, as no one ogled Pam's gravity-stricken ass anymore.

Across 62nd Street, Dangerfield's club sat hunkered down in the evening dark like a ghost from New York past. When Susan moved from Connecticut to attend N.Y.U. in 1993, city residents seemed older. Thirty-somethings with strollers toured Central Park, middle-aged businessmen rode the subways, and elderly couples sat on benches of the traffic islands dividing Upper Broadway. Now, in 2019, most people bustling along the sidewalks appeared to be in their twenties: Americans, Germans, French, Russians, Japanese, and Chinese. Did they know about old comedy clubs? Would they even notice when Dangerfield's vanished one day, a Duane Reade or Chase Bank sprouting up overnight in its place?

Susan met Vasily Kozlov at 5:30 on Friday in the lobby of the Grammercy Hotel. He looked near sixty, but retained a thick mane of silver, swept-back hair and furry black eyebrows. Surprisingly, he was quite charming. Vasily had read Baudelaire, Mallarme, Lorca and other poets Susan studied as a lit major.

"I am so enjoying seeing the Kandinsky at the Guggenheim," he said, "and the giant Balthus in the Met too." Vasily skewered politicians and complimented Susan's intelligence. She expected an entourage, but it would be just the two of them riding in a limo.

Initially, Susan felt trepidation. Preston Pompay owned a South Hampton beach house and loved to write checks for local benefits. However, she soon realized that the sprawling McMansion they parked outside of was in Hampton Bays, a sort of a western gateway to the official Hamptons. A destination that blue blood snobs would never deign to show their face in.

"Hampton Bays?" Susan attempted to squelch any condescension in her tone.

"Yes, yes." Vasily laughed. "Where the Russian mafia has found a foothold."

The party champagne and artsy conversation relaxed Susan by the time they nestled into the rear of the limo heading back across the Long Island Expressway to Manhattan. An intelligent man, that's what Susan needed. Though hopefully around her age and somewhat American.

When the car reached the web of intersecting highways in the vague borderlands between Long Island and Queens, Vasily said, "I will be paying you." He laid out five one-hundred-dollar bills on the seat between them, and Susan folded the money into her Kate Spade handbag. "Of course I will be adding of a tip." He looked her over. "I am hoping we can bring about a pleasant conclusion."

"What?" Susan asked.

"A termination of contentment."

"What?"

"An ending that is happy."

Susan's marriage flashed through her mind and she wedged into the corner of the back seat feeling queasy. "I was hired as a platonic companion. That's it."

"Yes, but here in America, money buys everything. Just be naming of your price."

Vasily began singing, mangling The Beatles. "I getting by with you helping my little friend."

"Please take me home."

"You are a... prude?" Vasily's face clouded up. "You are spinster?" He slid closer.

"Stay away!" Susan grabbed her lipstick pepper spray. "Don't make me spray you."

Vasily smiled ugly. "Dmitri, pull over." The limo screeched to a halt in the nebulous area beyond the Van Dam Street exit from the Expressway. Vasily shouted, "You will be getting out—now!"

Susan stepped into the unknown. She had never walked this part of Queens. No Manhattan resident ever did. One glimpsed it during cab rides to and fro JFK or LaGuardia with curiosity, with dread. It held the last vestiges of the dangerous 1970s New York, cars weaving through iron trestle supports below overhead train tracks like in *The French Connection.*

The weather hung humid and overcast, the smell of ozone heralding rainfall. Susan considered Uber, but her iPhone's battery hovered at a near death percentage. She hustled past windowless brick storage buildings, fluorescent-lit gas stations, rows of dilapidated townhouses and seedy two-story establishments emblazoned with graffiti yet dark behind sheet metal doors. She tried hailing a cab near the flow of traffic avoiding paying tolls by taking the Queensboro Bridge, but a fine misting rain descended and taxis displayed "off duty" lights.

Susan finally obtained a ride.

She hesitated outside her building in a trance. *Are you a prude? You're the perfect sexless date; it's not like Bill cheated on you,* ran through her brain. Circling. Coiling. Serpentine. The walkabout in the spritzing rain made her feel feverish. Susan studied herself in the dry cleaner's window by her front doorway, astonished. The reflection looked sexy—almost feral. Hair damp but not soaked, her face flushed, bra apparent through a wet blouse and jacket. Maybe it was the full moon beyond the scudding clouds or the judgmental voices jabbering in her head, but Susan knew she wouldn't get any sleep without help.

She entered Place Market. Empty.

Pete glanced up, expression cocky and assured. But something in her manner made his face leach of color, as if a friend he'd waved to turned out to be a questionable stranger.

Susan plucked Advil PM off a shelf and tapped on her heels toward the counter, staring into Pete's eyes. He retreated until his back pressed against the wall behind him. The wall made of atoms and quarks and unstable matter seemed the only thing holding Pete from falling backwards, from tumbling off the planet's surface then drifting out beyond the gravitational pull of Earth.

"What do you want?" His voice sounded odd, strained.

Susan rattled the Advil container.

"Take it," he said. "No charge."

She slipped it into her jacket pocket but stood still. The entire universe had shrunk into the little bubble they inhabited. Time slowed to a crawl.

"Well, what is it?" Pete acted like a thirteen-year-old boy, perplexed and awkward.

"Do you read books?" she asked. Silence. "Did Pete go to college? Does he know things? Poetry?"

"Yeah, sure…"

Susan leaned forward against the counter. Waiting.

INTERNAL DRIVE

"Your parents really named you Royal Morgan?" Lola asked as they sped north to Flagstaff on Interstate 17. "Kind of sounds like a type of rum."

"Yes, they did, but they pronounced it Roy-al. And my friends—"

"Called you Roy."

Morgan nodded, then steered around a windswept eighteen-wheeler swerving in and out of their lane. "Your name is pretty special too."

"Please don't sing the song." Lola smiled. "But thanks for the ride. I'm wondering though, what about your job?"

"I took two personal days," Morgan said. "Can swing down to Sedona afterwards, go hiking, clear my mind."

"So beautiful there, the red rocks and all those vortexes. I'm kind of jealous."

"Why Flagstaff?" he asked. "What do you do?"

"I collect broken things I find. Then reassemble them."

"Oh, like a junk artist?"

Lola sighed. "An environmental artist..."

Morgan had just met the dark-haired, early thirties woman at Compassion Corner, the chapel at Phoenix Sky Harbor. Totally unexpected; neither of them religious, but curious about a church inside an airport. She was from Barcelona originally. He told Lola Diaz how he planned to move to the desert or some remote wilderness, and that hadn't scared her off. During their conversation, he offered to take Lola toward her destination in Flagstaff. Morgan was nearly fifty and his job checking claims for Southwestern Insurance would end when the year ended. Downsized. His near future held the training of his replacement—joyous corporate stuff.

He gazed over at Lola in her remote passenger side world. Her face shifting, calculating.

"You mentioned going off the grid, tossing your phone, shredding credit cards. Cash only." She stretched her slender arms above her head. "That interests me. It's brave—"

"Really?"

"—or stupid. Like you're willing to throw it all away. Travel the back roads you missed while stuck in the business world, or to become a desert mystic." Lola glanced at him then away. "You could teach me things." A wedge of pine-stubbled mountains loomed to their north.

Morgan understood she viewed him like a curious object in a museum, not something buttered or glazed at a movie theater's concession stand. "The teacher and the ingenue." Hard to believe he'd ever been the younger man in any scenario.

He turned on the car stereo. A growling female voice brooded over a distorted blues riff, then broke into a shriek, returning to hoarse gravel, before punctuating the phrase with a falsetto yelp.

"You like PJ Harvey?" Lola cricked her neck.

"Sure, why not? I mean, we're around the same age."

She stared at the CD player then toward Morgan in disbelief.

He exhaled. "What do you expect me to listen to, Simon and Garfunkel?"

Her face went pouty. "I love them," she said. "My parents played me their songs when I was a child."

Morgan drove as Lola dozed off, curled in the passenger seat amid the September afternoon dazzle of heat. The old Honda Accord's AC sputtered, unable to cope. He felt dehydrated, dry as a cow skull planted out in the high desert.

Something about the wide-open stretches of land north of Phoenix reminded him of taking I-70 through western states. During his late-twenties, before both failed marriages, Morgan drove cross-country to California in 1997 with an older woman. A laughable term now. She was thirty-eight, looking youthful in her boyish haircut and expensive sunglasses. Almost like an actress from a French New Wave film, or the cute wife in a Fellini movie—traditional and family-oriented, but also eccentric with secret bedroom kinks. Only when his road partner removed her sunglasses could he read the mileage and worry around her eyes, could he see forty gaining on her fast.

They had dated for three short weeks in Manhattan when he revealed his mad plan of relocation. In the press of flesh, where common sense surrenders, she agreed to go along.

They went in his Volvo. She didn't like oncoming headlights blinding her at night, and it took a few hours for her vision to focus in the morning. So he drove. Morgan wanted to stay at basic chain motels; she preferred expensive hotels to luxuriate in hot baths, to draw out the journey and invest romance into weary corners. He chose to eat at Waffle House or an IHOP nearby the interstate. She groused, wanting to sleep late.

They laughed in communal solidarity at pickup truck hunters in flannel shirts and bill caps under the forested canopy of Pennsylvania. They stared puzzled at the three crosses by the side of the road sprouting here and there as they passed through Indiana and Iowa—feeling marooned in some earlier decade. The old Volvo's cassette player churned out mix tape songs while they lived endless hours of late marital boredom across the corn fields of Kansas and flatlands of Eastern Colorado. Until finally the Rockies reared up to show their awesome spectacle, brought depth and altitude back into focus.

Late at night in a Limon, Colorado motel, she insisted America would have been better off morally if George Bush had won the 1992 Election and Bill Clinton had remained in Arkansas where he belonged. For the first time on the trip, Morgan wished he could go back in time before meeting her, rewind the mix tape.

Nonetheless, they bonded, finished each other's sentences, made elaborate, impossible plans for when they reached California, and nestled together on a highway that seemed to stretch out forever. They chased one florid sunset after another—at least until their scenic detour in Utah. Near Moab, a deer sprung out between the massive red rocks canyoning the road. Straight ahead; the impact brutal. It was Morgan's only option besides straying into the oncoming lane and suffering a head-on collision with another car.

An entire life together lived in a single week. After they rerouted north with a dented hood and animal death haunting their silences, she took a plane from Salt Lake City back to her mother's place in New Jersey. They never met or spoke again. What was her name, Tina? Deena?

"Ground control to Royal Morgan." Lola prodded his upper arm several times. "You still here?"

"Huh?"

She brushed her long bangs from her eyes. "Thought I lost you on a stretch back there."

"Just daydreaming," he said.

"Did you leave them behind?"

Morgan's neck jerked. *Did she know about his past?* "Never left anyone behind."

"I meant your dreams, silly." Lola squeezed his tensed right shoulder as the sun tucked down low to the west. "You may as well stay over when we get to Flagstaff. Drive south in the morning." She paused. "You know, on the couch."

"Yeah, okay, maybe."

"Great," Lola said. "Hey, I'm a little short. Do you mind splitting the room?"

"I guess." Morgan felt a sudden urge to pull over and drop her off in the middle of nowhere, but he didn't. Morgan would forge ahead to whatever unsatisfying limbo lay beyond.

"Roy-al," Lola said. "That's a name I won't soon forget."

In a month, Morgan wouldn't remember her name, and if she recalled him at all, it would be as "some older guy who gave me a ride." Perhaps a certain value lay in interstitial spaces that led nowhere, rest areas between one's incessant struggle to thrive, to remind the world that you still existed. He played with the radio tuner, all static except an annoying country station. Left it on and thought of nothing.

"Something in the road," Lola shouted. "A coyote, or dog."

To the right was an embankment and no shoulder. They'd tumble and roll downhill. To the left he saw a massive FedEx double trailer truck advancing toward them—a hundred yards, two hundred yards? Hard to estimate in the heat vapors off the asphalt, the whole thing coming on like a surging death mirage. Or should he continue straight ahead?

This time, Morgan swerved left. If he could accelerate fast enough then brake on the far side of the lane...

He heard the piercing diesel horn mix with Lola screaming and realized it was good. They were still breathing then, and even that much life felt special, intense to experience. As close as he'd ever cut it just to avoid an animal who'd likely get hit later that day. Would his choice have changed anything decades ago?

The car decelerated on hardscrabble terrain beyond the highway. Lola was thrown forward, gasping for air when something rooted in the landscape stopped their juddering motion. Morgan listened to the drawl and twang of heartbreak emanating from the radio. He didn't want to get out and inspect the front of the Honda. Ever.

Maybe tomorrow, the day after, or a week from Friday, Morgan would reach the point where a person runs out of disappointments, has made every imaginable mistake, and then the good things begin to happen. Inspiration, exhilaration, the sense of an unknown love waiting somewhere out there just beyond the next ridge. All possible while you're alive.

MAKE THAT A DOUBLE

When Henry Kropf startled awake, his head throbbed and his body felt listless. Though fifty-seven for another week, Henry imagined himself as much older upon standing. Short-term memory fogged, a void. Dreams of running were all he could recall. Sitting back on the mattress, he ignored the damn landline ringing from their living room. Any time he suggested removing the phone, his wife Kelly defended it for emergencies. "If we lose cell reception or the power goes down, that line will still work." She had proven this truth during a Southern California Edison rolling blackout.

Was I drinking? Henry certainly smelled like a beast. All of it confusing. Over the past two years, he'd restricted himself to a single cocktail on social occasions, trying to be clear-eyed and present as he approached senior status. His father became an angry old man in his final decade, cursing the world no longer being the way it once was at some vague distant time. Henry felt resentments too, but endeavored to be friendly, to engage with restaurant servers, check-out clerks, and strangers he encountered. Offering money when he could to those camped on the streets. Because everyone was being pounded by a giant shit-hammer of rage politics, inflation, extreme weather events, and a general instability in culture.

Kelly crept in wearing a T-shirt and pajama bottoms; she tousled his hair. "You were an animal last night. I'm walking funny today."

Her words puzzled him. Of late, they slept in separate bedrooms and their monthly date night barely ruffled the sheets. "I'm sorry," he said. "I've blanked on the last twelve hours. I didn't mean to—"

"It was fantastic," she said. "I thought you'd lost interest." Kelly sank down onto his lap. "What got into you? Did you take something?" she whispered. "I finally sent you away so I could get some sleep." She flexed a wicked smile then rocked back and forth.

Noticing sensitivity, he shifted her weight off of him. Kelly's bedhead was a glorious tufted mess. She looked almost feral, or like an Appalachian girl clinging proudly to her disheveled youth. Light years away from Kelly's coiffed and glossed real estate agent persona.

"Have to go to work." He cracked his neck. "Who called?"

"Duke's Tavern. They found your debit card." She rolled her eyes.

Henry knew one thing. "I haven't been there since last month." Maybe he lost his card at a gas station or the post office and it got snatched.

"Normally, I'd be mad, but I just want to blast some Kate Bush and sing along."

"After I leave, please." He hustled for a hot shower.

Under the spray, Henry again considered disconnecting from social media. Arguing with old high school classmates on Facebook about politics had lost its charm. The Instagram parade of vacation photos and "I'm still hot" selfies no longer provoked interest, but more a stultifying boredom from repetition. *Is that all we do now?* he wondered. *Brag about traveling and declare our amazingness, over and over?*

A half-hour later, Henry lingered by their front door, studying the rusty, spider-webbed Porsche 911 someone had abandoned outside at the curb. Any whiff of retro cool negated by its Trump bumper sticker set right next to a Deadhead skull. Yet another item to deal with on his "to do" list.

Kelly lay sprawled across the living room couch, staring at their large flat screen. "I need to process last night," she announced, as if speaking to a therapist. "It wasn't normal for us. I was happy, but now I'm confused."

Still unclear on what had transpired, he replied, "Going to get my card and then to work."

Her attention remained on weather alerts from the East Coast. "We have a storm funnel and a bomb cyclone, followed by an atmospheric river," a harried remote voice said. "Stay safe," a female news anchor advised. Kelly repeated it.

Henry drove his Kia Sportage down Main Street of Santa Valeria. Pedestrians jaywalked brazenly, electric bikes hummed about, both with and against traffic, as youths on e-scooters rode the bike lanes while staring at their phones. *On the verge of chaos*, he thought. *Amazing there aren't more accidents*. As he squinted through sun glare at strip malls and plazas, a Ford Explorer cut him off without signaling. Henry honked then began deep breathing. *Let it go.*

In the perpetual twilight of Duke's Tavern—notorious for its stiff drinks and bland food—a manager greeted Henry, pumping his hand with late night enthusiasm at nine a.m. The label on his vest read *Chip*.

"Good to see you," he winked, "wild man."

"It's Henry."

"Whatever floats your boat." Chip ushered him past the dining area into their back office. A serious woman wearing black frame glasses sat doing the books, tapping on an old-fashioned adding machine, paper strips belching out of it. Both men took chairs by a desk.

"Apparently you had quite a party."

Henry rubbed his forehead. Early morning and all signs pointed to a day that would only get worse.

Chip slid Henry's debit card across the desk top. "You bought drinks for everyone at the bar. The bartender Elvira told last night's manager and they closed the tab at $400." He paused as if waiting for gratitude from Henry.

"Not me."

Chip cleared his throat. The walls held framed photographs of Dukes: John Wayne, Duke Ellington, Hunter S. Thompson, and the Dukes of Hazzard. "Here's the thing." Chip attempted a smile, but it sagged. "You signed the receipt Harry Krupp."

"My name's Henry Kropf."

"Your bank believed it was forged, the card stolen, so they reversed the transaction."

"I wasn't here yesterday."

Chip sighed. "My night off, but Elvira insists it was you, the guy who gets hammered every week and leaves with a different lady..." His voice tapered off. "I did not mention that to your wife this morning."

"Try and I'll sue for slander." Henry gazed around. "I come maybe once a month, have a single drink, watch football, then leave—alone."

"We're still short $400." Chip frowned.

"Someone stole my card so I'm glad Trace Bank denied payment." Henry stood. "I'm going there now."

"You do that." Chip rose, nodding. "But let's circle back, settle up by week's end, no?"

Henry strode across the dim lounge through a perimeter fog of Old Spice. Older men hunched over the bar, washing breakfast down with high-octane drinks, waiting for sports to animate the jumbo screens and give temporary structure to their aimless lives.

Just outside Duke's door lay an entryway alcove where customers smoked at night. This morning, a lone woman puffed a cigarette while staring at her phone. She wore evening clothes: black leather skirt, stockings, heels, a dark jacket, her sun-freckled cleavage heaving up through a spangled bustier. Henry crept by, intent on remaining invisible.

"Hey, wait a minute." She stabbed his chest with her index finger when he turned. "Don't you recognize me?"

Henry studied her. She had the familiarity of either a server or a Duke's regular, but not anyone he'd ever spoken to. "Sorry, you must be mistaken." He grinned. *Stay polite.* "I've never met you before."

"Right, daylight amnesia." She laughed in a harsh

wheeze. "Dirty Harry is what you called yourself. And jeezus did you live up to it. My ass still hurts." She winced.

"My name is Henry, and I'm married."

"I *know* that." She raised a fist to show a ring. "So am I. That's what made it perfect. No commitments, just some guilt-free fun."

Henry decided to play along. "No strings, exactly. It's history. Take care."

She punched his sternum. "You don't rock my world then ignore my texts. Debbie wants an encore."

Henry shook his head. "You're mistaking me for someone else. I'm old, I'm boring."

"Today you are." Debbie touched his brow. "Why you wearing your hair forward like that, Caesar? It was spiked up before. Don't hide your big forehead."

Henry made a dash for his Kia and exited Ocean Breeze Plaza. *Who was this married lookalike who chased the ladies, drinking all night?* It made him angry, then immensely jealous—that someone his age could live so dangerously and free. *You have your health and happiness*, he thought. But that didn't help at all.

As he navigated Main Street, the blocks blurred. Besides the palm trees, Henry's entire little coastal city had transformed into a generic slice of Anywhere, USA. Target, CVS, Verizon, Starbucks, Whole Foods. *Where did the old town go?* Quirky sewing stores, luggage repair shops, the board game center, used bookstores were unable to afford the ever-rising leases. Replaced by fancy jewelry emporiums and home design outlets, or not replaced at all. Nearly a third of Main Street businesses sat empty, waiting on big money companies to arrive and pony up the staggering rents.

Inside Trace Bank, he sidled up to an unfamiliar teller. Constant turnover. This employee clearly knew Henry as he inserted his debit card into the reader. "Dude. Welcome back." The bank bro gazed at a screen. "Happy birthday, by the way."

"That isn't until next week." Henry wanted to stay civil, but already felt irritation tighten his face. He hated that banks and doctors and basically everyone possessed all his personal information. Instead of receiving a birthday greeting from a longtime friend who remembered it, in the digital age, some rank stranger yelled it out as a business requirement. A crass corporate attempt to show humanity.

The guy with a *Brendan* name tag looked sheepish. "We're supposed to say it five days before or after, in case you don't come in on—"

"Sure, thanks." Henry nodded.

"No worries. FYI, your card's been canceled."

"It got stolen, used last night, then Trace must have shut it down." He paused. "Can you expedite me a replacement card, overnight it?"

"Totally, for a $30 trusted customer fee." Brendan leaned closer. "But dude, tell us another filthy joke." He eyed the neighboring teller, a young Latino with a wild explosion of hair. "They are so legit."

"Me? I'm no good at jokes."

"What?" the other teller, Victor said. Both employees scanned the bank, but customers were bunched by the ATM machine outside. "Your dank stories are fire."

"Yeah," said Brendan, "you're a legend, boss."

"I'm Henry Kropf."

Brendan squinted at the canceled debit card, then showed it to Victor. A strained moment passed. "Wow, could have sworn..." He tapped out a new card order on his screen.

"Sorry." Victor's eyelids drooped. "Please don't tell our manager."

Henry reviewed his recent account transactions. $15 spent at the Savoy Cafe yesterday at one p.m. *That's right. Must have dropped my card after paying for lunch. Then the scam artist grabbed it.* He withdrew $100 in cash to last him until the replacement arrived.

When he exited Mountain View Plaza via the ramp leading onto Main Street, there sat Ron. He drifted around town, but always wore a dangling cardboard sign strung around his neck. Clearly, another victim of hard economic times.

Henry braked, lowered his power window, and thrust three dollars outward. Someone once told him to avoid eye contact. Too personal, too judging.

"I like you better at night," Ron said.

"What?" The bills Henry held flapped in the breeze, useless.

"By day, you only give me money to feel better about yourself. To hide that you hate yourself." Ron spat. "You won't even look me in the face."

Henry accelerated over the sidewalk hump and lurched blindly into traffic, his head burning with rage, embarrassment, confusion. Nearby cars honked and swerved as the burly driver of a pickup truck gave him the finger.

Henry arrived at work by ten. Terminus International served as an umbrella company for a dozen insurance outfits, claiming to be independent arbitrators. They fielded calls from customers seeking better rates, adjustments in their coverage, to complain, and when it couldn't be negotiated, to cancel their policies.

He powered his laptop and Googled "Harry Krupp." The screen flashed before showing a 404 error message: *Page not found.* While Bing did find a Harold Krupp website listing, the link led to a 403 error: *You don't have permission to access this.* WTF? He hit the back key. Henry recalled seeing a lookalike of his younger sister while visiting Santa Fe, New Mexico. She wore similar black stretchy clothes, had the same hair and exact tilt of her head as she examined food labels inside Trader Joe's. He hovered nearby until she eventually spoke, gargling out double vowel words into her iPhone that sounded distinctly Scandinavian.

Brad Terdman pushed open Henry's office door moments after he'd shut it for privacy.

"Hey, man." Brad scowled. "So you're coming in at ten now?" His complexion was the dusky pink of boiled hot dogs.

"Just today." Henry's head rested in his hands. "Some personal matters. I'll work till six."

"Yes you will." Brad fancied himself a friend, though they never socialized. He perched on Henry's desk edge. "Listen, you can always share private stuff with me. Sure, I'm fifty and you're pushing sixty, but we're basically the same: older white guys who feel the country is going in the wrong direction, away from our Christian values."

"Wait, what?"

Brad's thick front hair was combed back over an oval swimming pool of scalp. He glanced through the cracked door to where receptionists talked in phone cubicles, then lowered his voice. "I had a colonoscopy last month." Brad's mouth twitched. "I was under Twilight sedation, but you get a printout and eight color images of the inner journey." He sniffed. "I'll show you later."

Henry coughed. "Um, I've got clients to contact." Luckily, his desk phone buzzed.

"Cheers." Brad winked then shut the door behind him.

Henry reclined in his leather chair. "Hey, Kelly. What's up?" He envied his wife selling real estate from home; no Terdman existed in her life.

"You used to call from work to tell me you loved me." Her voice sounded breathy.

"That was ten years ago." Henry spoke carefully. "I, I thought it was understood by now."

"Eleven years ago was the last time," Kelly replied. "And nothing is understood. I still don't understand last night."

"Right, but I'm slammed and need to return clients' calls."

"Someone in a hoodie was skateboarding outside on the sidewalk," she said, ignoring Henry. "I assumed a teenager avoiding school. So I yelled, 'no skateboarding in this neighborhood.' Said I'd report him." She paused. "When he turned, it was a person of color, in his thirties. He pointed at me and called me a *Karen*." Her voice trembled. "I voted for Obama, for Hillary, for Biden and Kamala. I. Am. Not. A *Karen*."

"Of course not. You're a Kelly."

Henry sensed that hadn't helped. "Listen, we'll eat somewhere expensive tonight." After the call, he remembered his limited cash.

Another line buzzed: a woman named Maria Hernandez. "My premium with County Farm just went up $700," she said. "I cannot afford it. Will you help find—"

"Yes, yes." Henry typed her policy number into his laptop and scrolled through companies who offered similar coverage. With gut-wrenching speed, he found that the cheapest quote was still $500 above her new rate. Henry died a little inside. The world had become a vice that tightened a bit more with each year—crushing hope. Home prices remained high yet sales were stagnant due to interest rates; apartment rents kept climbing with more demand and less available units. While premiums had risen with coverage not guaranteed. Homeowners were being turned down in areas affected by catastrophic weather events. After two minutes on his laptop, he knew Maria had inherited her parents' small cottage, raised kids, and worked long hours for a minimal salary.

"Hello?"

"I need time to compare rates," he lied. "I'll contact you tomorrow." Maybe he could wrangle her a loyalty discount.

"You will call back," she said, "really?"

"Definitely. My name is Henry Kropf."

"At County Farm, they have robots answer. I explain to them." Her voice broke. "They do not understand and transfer me, then I am disconnected." She sniffled. "When I tried Terminus, a man who sounded like you shouted and hung up."

"I'm sorry." The whole system was fucked. Human conversation now a rarity. A.I. had only exacerbated the awful corporate policies of outsourcing personal interactions to cold machines. "You *will* hear from me, Mrs. Hernandez. I promise." He disconnected.

A clicking sounded. "Henry, I monitored your call. Randomly, like I do with all agents." Brad Terdman exhaled. "Don't give false hope that you can't deliver on. We're advertised as independent," he said, "but we're dependent on a dozen companies. Make sure you switch homeowners to one of them."

"But none gave a better quote for Maria."

"Then share rates from hurricane and flood states that are way worse. Make her feel good about paying more. That's your job. We hired you for performative empathy."

"I want to help."

"We can't help anyone with inflation this crazy," Brad said. "Until our new leadership cuts all regulations and we get back on the gravy train we rode in 2019, our hands are tied."

Henry felt an urge to strangle his boss, but said, "I've another call."

During the afternoon, Kelly phoned again. "I want to have a child." She paused. "Henry, are you there?"

"Kelly, I'm turning fifty-eight and you're fifty." He knew facts wouldn't win the argument.

"Obviously," she said, "but we can adopt. A new chapter in our lives, so we're moving forward, not on a treadmill to nowhere."

His early morning headache pounded like a jackhammer migraine. "This is sudden, Kel. What brought it on?"

"Last night. We did it like strangers who met in a bar, and I liked that." She cleared her throat and Henry knew not to speak. "To be honest," she said, "I've been considering an affair. Not with anyone specific. I mean, you come and go after dinner. We sleep in separate bedrooms. We're housemates basically. Something has to bond us together for the future."

"Let's discuss it tonight. My bank card stuff delayed me, so Brad insists I work till seven." He finally convinced Kelly to let him go.

Brad's voice instantly sounded. "You were right, you *do* have personal problems."

"Jesus, Terdman. I can't believe you eavesdropped."

"It's pronounced *Tear-deman*," he said. "Anyway, it's a company line and I'm required..." Brad's voice trailed off. "Why doesn't Kelly call or text you on your own phone?"

"Because I don't answer that or respond." Henry needed private space inside his head.

"Aha." He sniffle-giggled. "I never said stay until seven, but I won't tell. The bro code."

After six, out in the parking lot, Henry Googled "Harry Krupp" on his iPhone. A 2015 death notice for a ninety-year-old Pittsburgh art dealer showed. Neighbors suspected him of serving in the German army during World War II. *Wait,* he thought. *Am I dealing with a Nazi's son?*

At JoJo's Lounge, blitzed regulars weaved by Henry, barely maintaining their equilibrium. The burning smell of charred meat, gristle, and grease spatter wafted over from the open kitchen's grill. He tucked into a circular Naugahyde booth where his longtime friend Gray Simon sat immersed in a paperback. "Thanks for meeting on short notice."

"Sounded like you were in a dark place," Gray said without looking up. "Card stolen, minor identity theft." He removed his reading glasses and set the book down. "We live in vexing times."

"Rereading *Steppenwolf* ?" Henry opened it. "The story of Harry Haller written by Hermann Hesse. Coincidence?" His friend laughed. "I'm running on cash tonight, so I'll just get a beer."

A man with dark dyed hair and a leather jacket stopped alongside their booth. "Dirty fuckin' Harry!" He cackled. "Teach me your methods, Sensei."

"Well, I..." Henry winced. The damn doppelganger had visited JoJo's too.

"Did I hear you could only afford beer?" His smile resembled a leer. "Hey, Eric," the stranger shouted to a bartender. "A Cyclone for my man." He glanced at Henry again. "Better make that a double. On me." A quick wave, then he sauntered off.

"I don't know him," Henry told Gray.

"Nor does he know they don't serve doubles. JoJo's regular drinks are deadly enough."

When a server deposited two Cyclones in fancy high glasses, Henry slid one across their table.

Gray rubbed his face. "So we agree that humanity is heading in a dark and dangerous direction—"

"And nothing we say will change its course by one iota. Cheers!" They both drank deeply. The Cyclone's mix of vodka, rum, and gin hit Henry's bloodstream fast. Best moment of the day. He closed his eyes—out—then eventually reopened them. "What happened?"

"You went to the men's room." Gray studied him. "Looked like you were sleepwalking."

"I don't get eight hours a night anymore."

"Have you tried gummies?"

"They didn't work, and I stopped taking Ambien," Henry said. "Wandered the neighborhood in my pajamas. Kelly found me asleep in the car one morning."

"Weird," Gray replied. "Anyway, events have spiraled beyond control." He flattened strands of his hair down from their mad professor stance. "Maybe we never had control, but there once was the belief if the public wanted guardrails on the development of A.I., then politicians would pressure tech leaders, who would obey them. No longer. Or if we chose to address climate change, then all humanity would agree our survival is a good thing. No, it became a red state, blue state debate. Another key issue to have it's back broken on the political divide." He drank and shuddered from the cocktail's potency. "Instead, while Congress does nothing, we watch tech companies develop whatever maximizes their profits and dominates market-share without giving a rat's ass about humanity, about you and me."

Henry scooped pico de gallo from a plastic cup to slather atop Irish soda bread. "As the real world becomes more chaotic, people retreat farther into social media, into virtual life, where they hold some slim lever of control."

Gray buttered a slice. "Yes, instant connection to strangers and our school friends. We're in touch, but also in argument. We meet in a jousting tournament environment, each trying to be the center of our internet ego experience. This detached contact actually isolates us further. Everyone is lonely now." He bit into his bread. "So we're on Facebook, Instagram, and whatever hellscape Twitter turned into. Over time, you slowly develop and mold an identity you present to the world. For us, that person is younger-looking, through an eight-year-old flattering profile photo. We catalog our funniest lines, best travel snapshots, and happiest moments in relationships that may closer resemble a roller-coaster than a sunset Cialis commercial. We begin to prefer the more attractive, wild, creative, funny character we've fabricated."

"Right." Henry tried sipping from his straw. Tasted almost like fruit juice that way. "As our real self ages, we avoid social interactions that were natural before. In Trader Joe's or Whole Foods, we pass someone we know online, pretending we don't recognize each other, both burning with recognition. We've been caught off guard, without our virtual world armor. We're not the person we've fooled ourselves to believe we are, and the truth is crushing. We desperately need personal exchange, human touch," he gripped Gray's shoulder, "authenticity. But we prefer the lie on social media platforms." He tore bread away from the crust. "We're doomscrolling toward oblivion."

Gray paused halfway through his tall drink. "Wow, that's strong." Perfumed women high-heeled past them toward the bar; one mouthed *call me* to Henry.

"Continuing the thread," Gray said. "Imagine if this social media personality we created got loose from the internet and bled into our real world. How would we compete with the glorious Frankenstein monster we brought to life?" He giggled from his words and intoxication. "Could we convince it to go back?"

"Our id run amok." Henry winced. "That's why I had to speak to you."

Gray flapped his hand as if dispelling smoke clouds. "You mentioned a double or doppelganger before." He smiled with disbelief. "Did you read Naomi Klein's book? I agree your card was stolen, and someone tried an identity theft scam, but I bet there's little resemblance. Easier to perpetuate these hoaxes than we imagine. People want to have faith in something nowadays, so in darkness, after drinks, a stranger with the right information, the correct words, and a bank card to back-up their bullshit, can probably fool half their intended targets. And Jesus Christ, that's enough." Gray finished his Cyclone.

"You doubt I have a lookalike?"

"They're potentially scattered across the globe," Gray said. "But they wouldn't want to impersonate you, or me. We're not rich or famous."

"So you don't believe in...the other?"

"The other *does* exist." Gray tapped his temple. "It lives inside us. Don't let it out." He clutched Henry's forearm. "I've papers to grade tonight. You're expected home too, no? She's texted me recently, concerned about you. I haven't responded."

"Yes. Thanks." Henry stood to help him put on his coat. "You totally depressed me, but I feel clearer too."

"Mission accomplished." Gray raised a hand in salute as he departed.

Leather man froze in mid-stagger and did a double-take. "Yo, I just saw you out back, Harry. How d'you sneak in so quick?" He shook his head before moving to the bar.

Leaving his suede jacket as a place marker, Henry dashed for the rear exit. Outside the heavy steel door sat a clearing bordered by strips of woods. Thin curtains of nature separated restaurants from business centers, and muffled a four-lane roadway churning in the near distance.

He was alone, but smelled recent cigarette smoke. Two men soon joined him. One short with greasy black hair, the other taller and dour-looking.

"Harry, remember me, Rudy? You owe $500. It's been two weeks." He smiled contempt. "Collection time."

"I'm Kropf, not Krupp."

"I don't give a crap." Rudy gestured at his large associate. He punched Henry twice, then knocked him off balance onto the damp soil. Darkness.

When he came to, the attacker was sprawled out, gazing back with fear. A purple bruise rose on his forehead and blood dripped from the man's mouth. No sign of Rudy. Henry's wallet lay on the dirt, emptied of the $100 and his driver's license. Car keys gone. A siren broke the silence. The big man groaned his way off the ground, then lumbered into the lounge. Henry saw a piece of firewood marked with red stains. The siren wail moved away south, toward his own neighborhood.

Unable to access the Kia, and with his phone still in JoJo's, Henry scrambled toward the woods, planning to travel home the hard way. Beyond the first scrim of trees, the ground plunged, descending into a dry riverbed. He stumbled over rocks, scraped against boulders, and muddied himself in areas still wet from the last rainfall. As his eyes adjusted to the night dark, he moved with confidence. A dedicated skelter. Then he tripped and face-planted. When he stood, the world spun around him. Rubbing his sore head, he touched a soft, wet wound. Henry stared at the dizzying stars above for a moment before collapsing.

He awoke running. Henry stuck to back streets, alleys, and vacant lots, only crossing busy intersections if absolutely necessary. When he finally reached the front door, his car sat parked behind the distressed Porsche at the curb. He could gauge the hell of his condition in Kelly's startled expression as she pulled him inside.

"I was worried, went to Terminus at eight." Her head slumped on his shoulder. "Then neighbors said you'd been taken on a stretcher to an emergency van. I checked Kaiser, but no Henry Kropf. Were you in an accident?" Kelly touched his wound. "What happened? Did you leave the hospital?"

She stared into his eyes, her own red and teary.

"I don't know exactly. But I'm not sure who I am."

"You promised to stop microdosing." Kelly's mouth sagged in disappointment. "What are you saying?"

"I'm not certain that was me with you last night."

She jostled him. "You're drunk, got in a bar fight, and now you're accusing me—"

"No, it's more complicated."

Henry wiped dried blood and dirt off his face with paper towels in their kitchen. "I have to find him, confront the impersonator."

"Who? I don't know what you're talking about."

"I need his secrets, then I'll make him disappear—for good." He wet his hair down. After removing the stained, filthy shirt, he soaped himself clean in the bathroom. "I'll be back."

"If you leave," she said quietly, "I'm staying at my sister's until you agree to couples therapy."

Henry barely registered her ultimatum. It was mano a mano; the original versus the other. Car keys sat atop their hall table. They didn't fit his Kia outside, but on a whim worked for the nearby weather-beaten Porsche.

At St. Matthew's lobby desk, he asked the night nurse for Harry Krupp.

"It's past midnight," she said. "Visiting hours are long over." She lowered her glasses as if Henry was a blurry lens hallucination. "You okay? Try tomorrow, when the doctor's on duty."

He shuffled along a corridor toward the bright cafeteria.

"Hey, wrong way, mister!"

Somehow Henry knew the metal door with a tiny window he passed led to the emergency stairs. Using a pen, he worked it open and climbed upward. He heard the swish of orderlies' scrubs and soft shoes pursuing him. Two men, determined. On the third floor, he scuttled down a dark hallway, where at the far end a corona of fluorescence glowed from a nurse's station. The attendants came bounding after him. He sprinted beyond the station until he reached Room 314. *Go inside.* From within, he locked the door and pressed his weight against it—waiting for battle. The men squeaked to a stop outside, then talked quietly, but neither tried to force entry.

Henry saw screen lights flicker amid the hum of racked machinery. A tall stand held a pouch of plasma with a tube descending while another device monitored heart rate. He pushed through the circular curtain surrounding the raised bed. It lay empty, though the top sheets were flung open and the mattress showed impressions of body weight. He listened to the beeps and drips, the almighty drone of an industrial fan in the distance, while feeling tired, so unwell. All those dreams of running finally catching up with him. *Best wait here for the doppelganger.* Henry climbed atop the bed, wrapped himself in the sheets, affixed the breathing tube to his nose, and relaxed, allowing the symphony of hospital equipment to lull him into a welcome sleep.

MEN OF GOOD FORTUNE

Miles Coburn had suffered through 1988. The slow-motion dissolution of his relationship with Debbie, the awkward beginnings of his band, watching former music heroes selling out to beer commercials, and strained relations with his mother. She wouldn't discuss his missing father and that only made Miles more anxious to know the truth. At twenty-four he felt adrift; still waiting for his adult life to truly begin. In retrospect, he would view 1988 as a golden year for concerts.

The last show he went to that fall was Leonard Cohen in mid-November. Miles took Joanna, his music biz friend's advice and bought *I'm Your Man*, listening to it religiously while catching up on Cohen's back catalog.

With Miles moving to his Village studio on December 1st, as a peace offering, he bought two tickets and invited his mother. Ali was delighted. She'd loved Cohen back in the seventies, but he fell off her radar until recently. Now everyone talked about the fifty-three-year-old poet, folksinger, written off by the music industry as a commercial failure, who had somehow crafted the best album of 1988, excoriating everything wrong about the synthetic decade of yuppie greed, covert wars, and cocaine mania. Something Dylan or no other artist seemed up to doing at present. Cohen's lyrics were both stinging and funny as hell.

"Thanks, Miles," Ali said as they walked the seven blocks down Broadway from her apartment to the Beacon Theater. "Is this your goodbye present to me?"

"I'm just moving to the West Village." He pointed south. "Only in New York would three miles away seem like a different country."

"I know things have been tense. I—"

"I get it," Miles said. "I didn't move out right after graduating. I fucked up my mailroom job at Warner Brothers. Instead of following you into the music business, I'm trying to start a band. And not even a commercial one that could actually make money."

"You burned some bridges at Warners, being part of that mailroom team. Bernie stole from the company, and Paco got some promotion guys to front him drug money, then ran off to Puerto Rico to build a church.'" Ali waved her hands in disbelief.

"To be honest, there was a ton of shady behavior there," Miles said. "The drug use, young secretaries who conveniently wanted to date the artists, the favors for radio people." He sighed. "Our mailroom crew was just the easiest to blame. Lowest rung on the ladder." Miles wrapped his plaid wool scarf tighter, the November temperatures dipping downward. "But, Debbie and I are done. It's definitely over. She went to Vegas with some lawyer and we had an ugly fight afterwards."

Ali frowned. "Miles, I try not to be judgmental, but I never trusted her." Ali put her arm in Miles's arm.

"Debbie would do whatever she had to do to get what she wanted. And she wanted a lot of things."

"I know, I know," Miles said. "When someone like that likes you, well, you want to believe it, want to just enjoy it. Then you try to ignore the signs when it turns bad."

"We all make bad choices, Miles."

"You mean like with my father?"

"Look." Ali pointed toward the marquee above the Beacon Theater: *LEONARD COHEN – In Concert.*

People swarmed around the entrance, their overcoats and faces bathed in the yellowy dazzle of lights from above. Most of the audience members appeared middle-aged or more, but Miles didn't care. He'd never fit in to whatever his generation was supposed to like anyway. Plus, Leonard Cohen made it seem cool to be older.

Joanna raced over kiss Ali on the cheek, then she lightly punched Miles's shoulder. "Tell me I was right about *I'm Your Man.*"

"You were absolutely, totally right."

Her whole face lit up. "Even the music snob looks happy tonight," she said. "See you afterwards. I have to go meet my, uh, friend." She hustled inside.

"Joanna looks really thin, Mom," Miles said. "The music biz powder diet. But you know all about that."

"Do you want to start an argument before the show? And do *you* really want to lecture *me* on drugs?" Ali asked. "I've done coke a couple times, but I don't go out to clubs and get high."

"I blame it for half the eighties bullshit. It infested the music world, the fashion business, and it's on Wall

Street. Drives the economy. Former radical hippies who became greedy yuppies use it as fuel, like your ex, Dorn. Lowlifes to high society, models and porn stars and Eurotrash, Democrats and Republicans, black, white, brown all come together on this one drug that boosts the ego, and triples the asshole factor."

"Let's find our seats," Ali said. "I hate when you get on a high horse. 'Let him who is without sin cast the first stone.'"

"Mom, you're an atheist."

"And Jesus might have lived longer if he'd been one."

Cohen's band played a blend of ethnic gypsy music, finger-picked folk, and Euro-pop, with Parisian monotone crooning in the Serge Gainsbourg tradition. Miles had watched Mick Jagger sprinting around stadiums in tight yellow football pants trying to prove he was two decades younger, while Leonard Cohen seemed content just to be alive. Standing center stage in his pin-striped suit and slicked back hair, vocal sirens Perla and Julie admiring him and echoing his gruff tones with their angelic voices, Cohen presented a mid-life crisis that any man would kill for.

He played a short first set ending with "First We Take Manhattan," then returned for an expansive second one, including Miles' favorite, "Tower of Song." It played like a European minimalist tribute to beatnik poetry readings over a bongo drum background. As if everything extraneous had been stripped away from the skeletal composition to leave only the magic heartbeat pulse and Cohen's breathy somniloquy remaining. The reverence of the crowd amazed Miles in their rapt attention to every witty lyric he intoned.

Ladies brought flowers to the edge of the stage to raise up to Leonard.

"He's got every older Jewish woman from the Upper West Side in the palm of his hand," Miles whispered.

'Watch it." Ali elbowed him. "I love seeing artists come back like this. It's inspiring." Ali's face held some religious rapture he'd never witnessed before. "Columbia treated Leonard like shit. He's a legacy artist who makes the label attractive to other talent. Reprise should have fought for him twenty years ago." She shook her head. "This is why I got into the business. It's the concert of the year, Miles. We're seeing an artist at his peak."

Miles felt elated. "Yeah, yeah."

After the show, they bundled up, said quick hello-goodbyes to Joanna and her surly-looking date. Miles recognized a figure on the Broadway traffic island. "Van Monk?" He ran over and hugged him. "This is what I was talking about when we argued years ago about—"

"Experiencing great art from the artists of your own lifetime," Van Monk interrupted. "I remember." He waved at Ali. "I have to go, Miles, but glad we were all there for Leonard."

Miles and Ali trudged up Broadway toward home. "Want some food?" she asked.

"Definitely, breakfast."

"At ten p.m.?"

"Of course."

Through both Van Monk and rock journalist Dustin Blazer putting in good words for him, Miles got his review of the Leonard Cohen concert published in *The New York*

Post. A couple of his paragraphs on the best concerts and albums of 1988 were printed in *The Daily News* between Christmas and New Year's.

Miles knew he couldn't make a living off snippets, but his friends dug it, and Ali framed his Cohen review. Though he enjoyed doing reviews, Miles had little interest in working his way up to writing band features. All that hanging out on tour buses, then either building them up as great misunderstood artists or tearing them apart as luck-blessed charlatans, held zero appeal to him. But Dustin promised him comped tickets to concerts if Miles would do him a favor when he needed one.

Miles agreed to the Mephistophelean bargain because, after years of record company perks, he felt weird asking his mother for tickets. However, with Dustin, you had to accept whatever favor he asked, otherwise he'd shut you out—close the iron gate. And Miles knew from Van Monk that a "Blazer favor" could be a major pain in the ass.

Dustin called him at two a.m. in mid-February. The call went straight to Miles' answering machine in his Thirteenth Street apartment, the volume on the plastic gadget set high.

"Come on, Miles. Pick up! This is your Uncle Dustin." Anytime he adopted a bogus familial bond, it was a sign he needed something. "I know you're there. It's the middle of winter and even the transvestite hookers on 14th Street are inside tonight." He paused. "I'm not going anywhere. I'm wired on some primo blow and I'll keep talking until this fucking tape runs out."

"Yeah, I'm here," Miles said, his voice still entombed in his throat. "Do you know what time it is?"

"The shank of the evening." Dustin laughed. "Remember, I pulled some strings? Well, I need that…"

"I'm not going out and buying you drugs tonight."

"No, no." Dustin sounded reassuring. "Want you to do an interview for me. I'm just too jammed up with travel and deadlines, but it has to get done."

"With who?"

Dustin paused, his breathing came loud through the receiver. "Lou Reed."

"You're joking." Miles hadn't followed Reed much beyond owning *New Sensations* from a few years ago and seeing his Honda motorcycle TV commercial. He did remember reading old *Creem Magazine* issues and the verbal slug-fests between Lester Bangs and Reed. "I can't. He'll laugh me right out of the room."

"No, man," Dustin said, "this is the new Lou. Have you heard *New York* yet? His best album in seven years. The guy is a regular human now."

Regular human being? Performers like Iggy Pop, David Bowie, Keith Richards, and Lou Reed could never be normal. Should never be. It was their alien, inhuman qualities that made them so fascinating. Did they ever eat, did they sleep?

"Lou lives in the countryside with his wife, a female wife," Dustin said. "He rides his motorcycle. Did you see the video for 'I Love You, Suzanne'? Lou danced like a motherfucker. I think he might have even smiled once." When Miles didn't respond, Dustin kept talking. "He's getting great reviews for *New York*, and I got seats for his St. James Theater run in March. This may be the best time in Lou Reed's whole career to interview him. The dude's actually happy."

"Yeah, okay. I guess so." Miles knew he couldn't refuse. Maybe Lou had changed. Hell, he must have—to have survived.

"Great, great," Dustin said. "Listen to *New York* beforehand. Impress him." Dustin paused, and Miles could hear him banging away on his manual typewriter. "Just remember Lou is sharp, whip-smart. Don't challenge him or bullshit him, just go with his whole new positive vibe."

The following week, Miles took a sick day at work and ventured down to Reed's publicist's office in SoHo at one in the afternoon. FM radio had been playing "Romeo Had Juliette" from *New York* and Miles enjoyed the album, so he looked forward to their meeting. Since the interview was set for two p.m. at Prince and Greene Street, he dropped in on Dorn Gallery east on Broadway.

"Miles, how's it going?" Frederick Dorn said. He held a phone crooked between his shoulder and ear, while he munched on a croissant. "How's your mother doing? No, not your mother," he barked into the mouthpiece. "Call you later, babe."

Miles studied his ex-stepfather. He wore dark suits with a gray t-shirt, showed *Miami Vice* stubble, slicked back his graying hair, and had a permanent sniffle.

"I'm downtown to interview Lou Reed."

"The walk-on-the-wild-side guy?" Dorn asked. Unlike Ali ensconced in the record business, Dorn had tuned out on hip music years ago. "He's still around? Good luck with that." Dorn was already calling other clients, selling, buying, counting profits in his head, figuring tax loopholes. His interest in art the only thing separating him from being a bland Wall Street broker. "Great to see you and give my love to your mother," he said as a means of dismissal. "Let's do lunch some time and catch up." Dorn waved goodbye then swiveled in his chair to have a heated exchange with someone.

Miles slurped up a bowl of onion soup at a French delicatessen on Prince before going up to the interview.

"You're three minutes late," a harried female helper said. "Please wait in the office." She closed the door behind him. The publicist's office had been decorated like a shrine to recent Lou Reed. All eighties photos: Lou on a motorcycle, Lou with his wife, Lou wedged in-between record company executives, his last few album covers framed on the wall. No freaky old shots of skeletal blonde Lou or pudgy Lou in glam makeup. Miles waited twenty minutes.

A compact man with a huge presence walked in wearing a black leather jacket and impenetrable shades. Reed's curly hair hung long in the back and had been cropped shorter in the front. His complexion looked gray, most of the flesh tone leached away.

Reed removed his glasses to take Miles in. His eyes were dead, mirthless.

This was the happy Lou? Miles switched on his cassette recorder.

"So who are you again?" The songwriter stared at a piece of paper on the desk frowning.

"Miles Coburn. Dustin Blazer asked me to do this interview for him..."

"For him?" Reed sniffed. "I insisted he *not* do the interview. Do you know what he said about me twelve years ago?" He sighed. "It doesn't matter." Reed put his shades back on. "What are you, twenty-two? You've reviewed a Leonard Cohen show. Wow."

"Twenty-four."

"Liberal arts college graduate, probably from the Upper West Side. Maybe Jewish, no, half-Jewish." Reed laughed in a self-congratulatory way. He gazed at his watch with a bored expression. "Let's see if you know anything. Okay, so what are your favorite records of mine?"

"*Transformer*, *Berlin*, the new one, and *Loaded*."

"Hey," Reed said. "Didn't you read the rules? Mary?"

His frightened assistant rushed into the office. "Yes?"

"Rule number one: no mention of my former band." Reed glared at Mary. "Did he see the guide sheet?"

"I sent it to Dustin Blazer, Mr. Reed. Maybe he didn't pass it on."

"Okay, you're not helping me here." He waved her away.

Reed faced Miles again. "Everybody says *Transformer* is their favorite, so you shouldn't." He paused. "*Berlin* was a masterpiece but nobody got it. I was pillaged by the critics. But my best was *Metal Machine Music.* Do you know why?"

Miles shook his head, figuring silence was best.

"Because I bridged heavy metal, experimental music, and classical music. People didn't understand it and RCA marketed it like a rock record. The most returned album in their label's history. How would you like to live with that? Oh, never mind."

"Can I ask about your band on *New York*?"

"Ask."

"You've used Fernando Saunders on bass for several years. Some people would say he's an odd choice for your style of three-chords-and-poetry rock."

"Some people are assholes. What people? You need to be specific if you're going to be a... journalist." He said the last word with contempt. "Why do *you* think I work with Fernando?"

Miles thought carefully, then remembered something from *Creem.* "You were a fan of Stanley Clarke's bass playing and fusion jazz, so you wanted a fretless bassist with that level of musicianship in your band."

For a slight instant, Reed smiled, then his lips flatlined. "You're pretty young to know that shit. You read it somewhere, an old interview." He leaned forward. "How do you know I didn't lie to Lester Bangs? You think that bastard deserved the truth?"

"No one would pretend to like fusion jazz, especially not the Godfather of Punk."

Reed jolted in his seat. "I hate that fucking name. Makes me sound ancient, and like I'm responsible for all that noise. My influences are Delmore Schwartz—look him up—Bertolt Brecht, Dostoevsky, and doo-wop."

"Back when you started in that other band in the mid-sixties, was your vocal style influenced by Dylan?"

"Ha-ha-ha." Reed put a hand to his head. "I love Dylan. Even his last album that everyone hates is better than most people's best, but you need to do research. Dylan started recording before me, in '62, but when did he start elongating his syllables? When did he start doing that talk-singing thing?"

"On *Highway 61 Revisited*?"

"More like *Blonde on Blonde* in '66, after he hung around the Chelsea Hotel and met Nico and Edie Sedgwick, after he saw me and the Velvets in concert, and after he heard our first album." Reed sighed. "Understanding history is *so* important. Okay, last question. Let's keep it current."

"Is this new album part of your happy, mature phase that began with *New Sensations?*

Reed made a snorting noise. "Please leave this office right now."

"It went well," Reed's assistant told Miles on his way out. "You got through a dozen questions and he didn't start screaming at you."

"Mary!" Reed shouted from beyond the closed door. "Get in here—now."

Miles exited the building and checked his cassette recorder to verify it had actually happened, then wandered north on Broadway toward Tower Records. He had a few choice words for Dustin Blazer.

ALMOST GRAND JUNCTION

Just beyond the Grand Junction city line on I-70, Pancake Palace does good business. It can't compete with Village Inn, and price-wise, McDonald's remains the cheapest, but it's popular—open from seven a.m. to eight every night. The Palace has a serious blue collar local following. People wait for it to open, smoking cigarettes outside in the cold Colorado morning air, then return later for a gravy-drenched dinner.

She has worked there as a server for a year. Keeps quiet and does her job, but feels displaced. Customers are used to her now, unlike the early days. *Hey, where you from? I mean, originally. This colder climate bother you?* Just nod to agree; act like your English is limited. Do what your told, keep your head down, and don't make eye contact when you smile—as you've been instructed to. Trouble is, if you smile while looking at a man directly, they take it as interest. How sad that no one smiles at them. Not their friends, their coworkers, or their wife. Starved for admiration, but all they get for their hunger at the Palace is flour, sugar, starch, and grease.

Her salary pays the rent, but not enough to replace her brokedown car. She yawns her way to the bus stop in the post-dawn chill, stamping her feet then digging frozen hands deep into torn jacket pockets. It's on the old highway, called the "business route," that runs five miles east and west of town. Past construction supply lots, sheet metal warehouses, rusted pumpjacks in constant see-saw motion. In the distance, piercing the horizon, snow-capped mountains linger—even in spring. Each day a repeat, same as the last. No promotion awaits, no doorway into a regular American life of a car, house, a backyard. Marriage not on the radar in her early twenties. She's received proposals both single and attached men, but none involved matrimony. Typical for servers.

Elmer of Grand Junction Mining once told her, "I got no problem with you."

"How do you pronounce your name?" Jordan from Southwestern Energy asked.

"Lakeisha."

"Really? Where you from?"

"I like America." *Pretend not to understand.* "May I take your order?"

Eggs and bacon, stacks of pancakes, Belgian waffles, oatmeal and brown sugar, cinnamon French toast, omelets, tuna sandwich with coleslaw, ham on rye, grilled cheese with tomato soup, BLT, club sandwiches merging into biscuits and gravy, meatloaf, chicken-fried steak, burgers and fries, open face turkey, and fried chicken. Immortalized in photographs on their laminated menu.

Vera, self-appointed queen of the servers, calls her "Lak," claims her name is too hard to pronounce. Somewhere in her fifties, Vera is tough and watchful. "The younger servers and line cooks are stealing my tips. Supposed to be pooled in that big juice pitcher then split up later." She keeps an eagle eye on it, sometimes marking the level of bills and change on the clear plastic with her lipstick.

"I seen Jordan talking to you, Lak," Vera says today, in the outdoor alley where they take fresh air breaks from the grill's eternal sizzle and spatter. "He hasn't asked me out lately." Vera presses her index finger's artificial nail into Lak's breastbone. "Just take his order. Out of all our regulars, Jordan makes a decent salary, could be my next husband." She stamps out a cigarette near her foot. "My first was a machine operator..." Her voice trails off. "Lost Ted in a rotary drill accident. Life ain't fair." Her eyes water. "I deserve a break, so don't get in my way."

Lakeisha traveled up from Albuquerque with Isabella and Melodina, all having faith in divine providence. When Farmington didn't work out, Isabella decided to try Phoenix—too hot—while Melodina set off for the East Coast. Left Lak to drive north alone on 550 then I-70 until Grand Junction was the last city left in Colorado to grab onto.

To pay her rent and save for a new car, Lak works from 8 a.m. to closing. Life away from work is fleeting. She runs at it and it runs away faster. Never enough time to do errands or buy necessities; just eat, sleep, wake up, and go back. She can't escape Pancake Palace, not even in her dreams.

The line cook Chuy sings during breaks. "You look so pretty today," he says in a high, reedy voice. Explained his name is pronounced "Chewy." Lak's only real friend at work. "Move soon, okay? Denver is better for you." The kitchen staff offer her rides at night, but she prefers the bus with no demands, even if their demand is only for conversation. Sometimes, if it's snowing or crazy windy, she agrees.

"Since my wife died, I could use help around the home, Laquinta." Carl, a needy regular, squeezes her hand. The contrast of his seventy-year-old, weathered rancher skin to her smooth skin is quite jarring. "You'd just cook and clean, give me hot baths and back massages. My sciatica has been acting up."

"Thank you, no thank you." She smiles while staring at the tabletop.

Carl's face prunes into wrinkly lines. "What do you mean, no? I'd pay you more than whatever you make here." He nods at his generosity.

"Liver and beans today? I'll put in your order." She hurries off.

"No flirting with the diners." Frank the manager observes everything from his perch at the counter by the cash register. "Keep it moving, Lakeisha." He slaps a newspaper against her backside. Later, when the rush dies down, Frank says, "Some customers mentioned your name. I told them you were most likely from south of the equator. Am I right?"

She points toward the back door to signal her break.

A half-hour after closing, the Palace is mopped and clean, with Frank reviewing receipts in his tiny office scented by the neighboring restrooms. Once outside, she rushes through the cool mountain dark toward the bus stop. A throb of lights from Grand Junction sparks a brief magnetic energy that doesn't linger. For they don't represent nightclubs or baseball games, nor outdoor concerts or county fairs, but car dealership lights, airport runways, and the dull parade of traffic lamps navigating the city's business route.

There it is, idling a hundred feet ahead, gray exhaust puffing up, the engine grumbling back into activity. Lak waves her arms in the air as she runs. The bus lurches forward in a few stuttered coughs, then into solid motion. She shouts and signals but to no avail. It must be Rashad the usual night driver. Another displaced soul, who wears glasses with thick lenses. Just making eye contact with him causes dizziness and threatens a headache. When Rashad gazes into the rear-view-mirror, he must see a distorted soup of images.

Lak's raised hands plunge to her sides like dying birds. A weathered blue Suburban screeches over. "Missed your bus?" a thirtyish man under a baseball cap asks. She recognizes him as a regular, but has never served him.

"Seen you working the Palace," he says. "My wife Bethany and I are heading to Grand Junction. Hop in." She hesitates, the wind buffeting her. "We're Christians," he adds. "I'm Jacob."

She climbs in back of the long vehicle amid smells of beer and tobacco, while modern country music plays loudly. Lak listens but doesn't understand why having lips that taste like Sangria could be a good thing.

Bethany stares at Lak without speaking. Features so bland and blank, like a pallid cult follower. "My child will be called Caleb," she eventually announces.

Behind in the Suburban's spacious rear are cardboard boxes and guns: rifles, shotguns, a pistol, and a military-style weapon. Sensing her curiosity, Jacob cranes his head around. "I like to hunt." He grins brown, chaw-stained teeth.

Lak wishes he'd concentrate on driving. "So many," she says. "Is there a war in Colorado?"

He laughs. "No, but we have to be ready."

"For what?"

"Well, nothing personal." Jacob clears his throat. "There's people from other countries want to sneak in, take what's rightfully ours. If it comes down to it, I'll defend me and mine."

"They are coming to fight you, steal from you?" She doesn't understand.

"Listen, I picked you up because that bus driver ditched you. He comes over from Saudi Armenia and steals a job from us citizens."

"You want to be a night bus driver?"

"No." He coughs. "But what if I needed to be someday? He'd have my job already. That stuff can't go on."

Lak notices they've reached the outskirts of Grand Junction, a quarter-mile from her small apartment. "Please, I can get out now, thank you."

"Come to our church meeting," Jacob says and Bethany—still facing her—nods. "It's an outreach program. We'll sponsor you."

"No, I can't—"

"Members get work and food. If our community trusts you, can depend on you, then nothing bad will ever happen."

Lak is puzzled. "What do you mean bad?"

"The Great Replacement," Jacob says. "We need you on our side."

"It's not your fault," Bethany says quietly. "The money changers are using you."

When the Suburban halts at a stoplight, Lak twists the door handle and bolts outside.

"Wait, you owe us for the ride," Jacob shouts. "Crazy bitch, we tried to save you."

Lak doesn't understand Americans who announce they're Christians. She wants to have faith in some higher power, but privately, so she rushes sideways as their car is forced onward with the stream of traffic. Two more blocks and her complex looms ahead. To avoid the nosy neighbors giving her suspicious glances, she climbs the stairs to her apartment in near silence.

The vigilant apartment manager soon hovers in her doorway. A tall man with terrible posture, Adam scratches at his sparse hair and moves his mouth around as if enduring dental discomfort. "Uh, Laquila. Starting next month, your rent's going up $200."

"In two days?"

"I shouted it up to you three weeks ago. You might not have heard me."

"It's hard to afford now." She gazes away to hide her thoughts.

"Not my decision," he says. "Came down from management."

As far as Lak knows, there's no company. He *is* management. "I will find another place."

"Good luck." Adam rubs his protruding belly. "We're tolerant here, but most won't even consider you."

"Why?"

"Well, you're not a, native Coloradan." His forehead scrunches with deliberation. "Maybe we can work something out. I need someone to do stuff for me."

She doesn't like how Adam's eyes bulge. "I am very busy at my job. Will tell you soon." Lak closes her door as he tries to insert himself further. "I am tired. Please, goodnight."

She wakes at 6:30 for a shower, breakfast, and to allow for the variations of bus travel time to work. Just before eight at Pancake Palace, she is dressed in their server uniform and fastening her hair back.

"We're switching sections today, Lak," Vera says.

"Frank told you this?"

"I've got seniority here, so I make the call." Vera frowns. "The tip jar's been falling lower." She wears a visor emblazoned with the Palace emblem; her permed hair puffed-up above it like gray-blonde cotton candy. "I'm better with the Mormon customers visiting from Utah. I'll make us bigger tips and get to wait on my future hubby Jordan too." A wide grin shows pinkish lipstick smeared onto her rabbity front teeth.

"I need a new place to live," Lak says. "Maybe above your garage?"

"Sorry, that little apartment is saved for my aunt when she visits." Vera sighs. "I will pray for you though."

Lak hears people offer "thoughts and prayers," but doesn't understand what that means. Thinks it's just a saying when someone doesn't know what to say.

She waits on the booths toward the west side, where the vinyl flooring has warped. Regulars prefer this section. They can stare off to the red sandstone mesas of Colorado National Monument fifteen miles away. Some male diners light cigarettes and must be reminded by Frank to tamp them out. Still living in the past century. They order coffee, maybe a muffin, and wait—until Frank shoos them along—for a job that never materializes, or a wife who left and hasn't come back. The longer Lak works there, the more she sees the harsh topography of the high desert written across their faces.

Today, a woman slathered with makeup sits across from a dour man and beams at her. Strange to see someone so done-up early on a weekday. On Sundays, families dine all groomed and dressed for church. Maybe she's in real estate. Lak can't tell if she's in her late forties or fifties, whether the glossy makeup makes her look older or younger, or just weird.

Lak takes their order, and when they are done eating, the woman beckons her over. "We've been noticing how attractive you are... Well, in general." The grizzled man watches from under his red trucker cap. "I'm Wanda. We could really use you for a business opportunity."

"Sorry," Lak says. "I am not a house cleaning person, thank you." Though she wonders if she should be with her looming rent situation.

Wanda gives a husky laugh, while her partner rolls his eyes. "No, no," she whispers, glancing at nearby booths. "It's for my husband, Bob." Wanda elbows the man. "He likes to watch."

"Watch movies?"

More mannish laughter. "No, honey. You and me, you know. We'll pay."

"Love me some strange," Bob says.

Lak reads faces and intent well. "Thank you, no. I will bring your check." She notices the woman scowling, her husband reddening with anger. After adding up the bill at the counter, she turns to Frank. "My break is now. Would you bring this to Booth #4, please?"

Frank slaps down the sports section. "Yeah, okay, but ten minutes. No longer."

Lak makes it out into the alleyway feeling faint, gasping for air. Chuy's happy presence makes her feel better—the harshness of the world unable to phase him. Perhaps sensing her tension, he hugs Lak. "Is okay, is okay."

Chuy sings old Spanish songs, his high voice sometimes breaking into falsetto. Frank and Vera believe he's gay, but Lak lived in Mexico years ago where she knew similar men—theatrical and effeminate. Chuy is very protective; the best thing about working at the Palace.

"I have to make more money. My rent is going up $200."

"Oh, no." He strokes her hair. "Chuy would let you move in, but I share an apartment with Pedro and Rolando." He lowers his voice so the two cooks don't overhear. "They are disgusting. Our bathroom is unbelievable."

"Don't know what to do."

"I told you before, go to Denver."

She nods.

"More open, for you, for me. They no judge." Chuy takes her hands in his. "Until then, I will give you my tip share."

She wants to cry. "No, I have to make money myself."

For a moment, Chuy seems sad, then he begins singing again.

At closing, Franks summons Lak into the cramped office. "I've gotten complaints about you flirting with customers." He stares at his desk. "I ignored them. Some of my regulars are kooks. But today, a couple told me you asked them for money for services."

"No, no, they want to pay me to go with them to their house."

"What? They plan to invest in my restaurant and are church-goers, so why would they lie? Anyway, the customer is always right." Frank counts out five hundred dollars, slides it toward her, then looks up. "I've got to let you go—tonight."

She exits the diner stunned. Overwhelming darkness ahead, the gaudy neon piping of the Palace glowing behind, of her past. Seeing the *Out of Service* sign at the local bus stop, she wanders homeward, numb to the chill, cocooned in her own thoughts. Family had warned her life in America would be difficult, but it had to be better than poverty-encrusted islands, than working in Mexico. Jets blink by overhead as she trudges along, feet weary after an hour of tramping the three miles. Ignores cars and drivers' cat calls to her.

"New rent is due tomorrow," Adam shouts as she climbs the groaning staircase.

Nothing of value in her studio. The bed, tables, and desk part of the furnished apartment. Lak packs a bag that she can strap over her shoulder and departs at 10:30

for the Greyhound stop. Time to leave Grand Junction forever. Without the energy to walk an additional two miles, she tries to hitchhike. Lak waves away an older bald man with beady eyes, then gets into a van where two young couples greet her happily. Beards, long hair, old clothing, maybe living in the van. Modern hippies are different.

"So, can you throw in some gas money for the ride?" The driver asks after a minute, his eyes red and twitchy.

"Is $5 okay?"

"Sorry, no. Everything you got." He laughs long and ugly. "Alethea, search her stuff."

Lak can't escape; they're driving too fast. The other man slashes open her carry bag with an Army knife. Alethea smells of body odor and clove cigarettes while she rifles through her things. She finally digs out the five hundred and her face shows both sorrow and guilt. Before the men notice, she shoves a hundred back into Lak's bag, then holds the wadded bills up high. The others cheer and whoop.

The driver swerves across to the shoulder. "Get out, and don't hitchhike. It's dangerous."

Lak gives the roadway wide berth, moving slowly until she rests on a low wall encircling an Enterprise car lot. Catching the bus impossible now. A high lamppost blinks on and off, casting splashes of unwanted fluorescence upon her.

When a big jeep pulls over nearby, Lak fears it's the police. A lone man in a tan suit emerges. He is perhaps South American or Mexican, handsome and clearly prosperous. "You work at Pancake Palace, right? What are you doing here?"

"I was robbed. Can't walk any farther to the Greyhound stop. Please don't have me arrested."

He sniffs. "No, I'll give you a ride." He glances at his watch. "We need to hustle for you to catch the 11:30 bus."

"I'm scared."

"Don't worry, sit in my back seat alone. I'll be your chauffeur." He strolls toward the vehicle.

Lak follows but hesitates on the door handle. "I-I…"

"You have to trust someone, sometime." He folds into the driver's seat.

She tucks into the back, pulling the sliced carry bag that leaks socks and underwear along.

They drive in silence with radio music playing until reaching the stop. The bus gasps smoke in the cold night air while passengers climb aboard. "Where you from?"

"My parents are from Haiti. Me? I remember Cuba, Bogota. Traveling always." Lak's mouth is dry. "I only have enough for a ticket or a place to sleep tonight."

He hands her a fifty-dollar-bill. "You heading for Denver? It's about $45 one-way. Stay at the YWCA until you get settled."

She is suspicious. "But I can't do anything for you."

"I did you a favor, that's all." He shakes his head. "The money's a loan."

She lingers just outside the jeep. "How will I pay you back?"

"In America, you'll always meet someone worse off than you, on the worst day of their life." He pauses. "Give the money to them, okay?" He stares into space. "When I first came to California, I lived in the culverts, cement waterways outside Los Angeles. Now go get on your bus." He shifts gears then motors off.

The bus driver makes a sour face at her distressed luggage, but takes the $50 and nods. Lak collapses across the last row of seats feeling warm, feeling safe. Isn't sure what lies ahead except that the worst is behind her. She sleeps through the six-hour-journey, oblivious to passengers jostling by for the restroom. The soft glow of dawn lighting the massive Rocky Mountains wakes her into a new world of beauty and possibility. She doesn't trust it yet; squeezes her eyes closed again.

IF YOU CAN JUST GET ACROSS

If you can just make it across 35th Street to Sixth Avenue, then you can meet Sarah. How long has it been? Did you ever really know her, or is that just some Facebook memory illusion? Get with technology: variable algorithms, the interlacing of codes. Same schools + enough mutual friends = a vague past relationship. Jesus, go already.

But you're still marooned on the east side of Fifth Avenue waiting for a break in traffic. A lone, orange safety cone sits by a trash bin signifying what? Caution? The whole street, the entire area is a fucking disaster zone.

Merge with the build-up of humanity lined on the corner, anxious, preparing to launch toward the far sidewalk. Grim-faced blondes in baseball caps and yoga pants lunge like gazelles, tour groups mass around trinket stores while their idling bus sulks at the curb, and steam billows from manholes to ghost the faces of passersby with ancient subterranean hobo funk.

"Holy shit, look!" People crane their necks amid the burning pretzel smoke to spy the Empire State Building thrusting vertical above the forest of buildings. A subway rumbles below, vibrating the asphalt—nothing is stable—the smell of grilled meat wafting up in dank courtyards from Korean restaurant kitchen exhaust fans, and listen deeper for the god-like "om!" hum of the much larger industrial fans mounted atop World War something-era brick hotels.

Men in suits run in comfortable shoes to catch buses already tilting away from their stops and turning precipitously onto narrow streets. Dodge around the plywood sheets stacked for no apparent reason, beyond the workers loading mattresses into storage areas, and a dedicated soul rummaging through garbage, as girls in leggings pass, and students parade in black rim glasses, three jeers to the goggle-pated fuck-face, the dumb-ass white guys yell provocations from a packed car speeding by. "Seriously, who still wears leather jackets?"

High-heeled ladies in short skirts stride with muscular thighs and black women sprouting dyed blonde hair that shows dark at the roots, ignore the karaoke bars pumping out '80s songs from behind fogged windows. Is there a crowd? Is it empty? *Don't you want me, baby?*

Irish pubs blast classic rock and doormen wave aimless cruisers inside for happy hour specials on well drinks. But their attempts are wasted on people texting, shouting into speaker phones, dodging and weaving around one another. Distracted. Don't gawk at the man in a tank-top with a non-ironic mullet or he will wear your teeth as knuckle rings.

Tourists roll heavy luggage and their facial expressions wonder, is this a vacation or a punishment? The thundering surge of traffic stops at a red light but three kamikaze bikers speed through screaming at pedestrians crossing in their way. Pedicabs dodge—for the moment—their imminent destruction by a swerving bus, long rows of garbage bags sit waiting for Godot, seedy men chewing toothpicks hand out cards to secret palaces of pleasure, or some DJ rave way-the-hell-out in Brooklyn. A female traffic cop admonishes jaywalkers while signaling to oncoming cars. Some people wear short-sleeve shirts, others are in down jackets, because one minute it's humid spring and the next, a cold wind nags at you like an angry ex.

You realize that this area of Sixth Avenue is now Koreatown because you saw it on a street sign, and Chinatown already exists miles to the south. There are Japanese and Chinese and Filipino and Vietnamese and Korean strollers, and you will never understand a single one of their languages in your short human lifespan. But they are all shopping and talking and rushing through their lives and seem to have the money to thrive in Manhattan. European families stagger out of swinging glass doors to hotel lobbies, carting enough baggage for a month, past the Middle Eastern T-Shirt, gewgaw, souvenir emporiums that seemed to have multiplied during your visit.

Sarah? You see someone resembling her ahead and you close in—too close—only to shock the stranger. Everyone is clustered tight in Greeley Square, but never ever touch them. Don't nitro their glycerin. And the noise of diesel horn honks, the shriek of brakes, the oppressive hallelujah of sirens, and foreign conversations all blot out the pings. So when you eventually stop, a hapless stationary man among the jostling movement of hundreds converging on your point, your momentary inconvenient space in their universe, you find that she has texted.

So sorry. Almost broke my leg. I should really see a doctor. Hope we can meet on your next trip.

You are left staring at a gigantic Victoria's Secret video display, sexy yet robotic, wondering where you can find a small bottled water for under three dollars? But you're already drowning and lost in a place once familiar where time's passage has rendered you a stranger. Let the current drag you with its whims, for struggling in the riptide only brings misery. Throw away plans, recede back to the tide pools and observe. Smile. Youth is eternal as long as you don't try to hold on to it, or claim it for yourself.

Some friends never planned to see you at all, but rather hoped to text locally. Like Brad.

Great to know you're in town, man. Come back soon. Drinks next fall?

LONGER BOATS

Grant Peterson felt summer dying all around him that Friday. Just Labor Day weekend before school began, the rest of the year a slog of numbers and dates and reading assignments.

"Grant," his mother said during the ferry ride to Nantucket Island. "Apparently, there's only one room at Jared Coffin House." She gently touched her sprayed, upswept hair that looked ready to launch from her head. "So you'll stay at Uncle Raymond's."

Raymond wasn't Grant's uncle, more a godfather. But his two daughters, fifteen and sixteen, regarded Grant as a boy hobbled with being a mere thirteen. They were tall and developed, and gossiped and dreamed of high school seniors, or really old guys in college.

"We'll meet you for lunch," his mother continued, "or possibly dinner."

"Remember," his father said, "summer's over, so have some damn fun." When Grant didn't reply, his father added, "I wish I could relax this weekend instead of going to boring dinner parties and club lunches—"

"Edward..." Grant's mother interrupted.

On the outer decks, large American flags whipped in the breeze, acknowledging the Bicentennial. 1976 signified just another year to Grant, though he felt certain his teachers would use it to prompt essays and projects through December.

Rolling off the ferry ramp, Grant's father drove their rented AMC Pacer west on Madaket Road until he yawed north on Eel Point Road to Uncle Raymond's cottage: a cedar-shingled, unpainted wood structure turned gray from the stormy coastal winters. Unlike the historic homes downtown, it was a sprawling single-story that sat on a cliff. A wooden walkway outside became a stairway descending over the rise and through dunes to the beach.

"Thanks again, Ray." Grant's father pumped his friend's hand. "See you and Sandra tomorrow at lunch." Raymond had divorced and now dated Sandra Wallace, a close friend of Grant's parents. A rumble of ignition and a belch of exhaust left Grant alone.

Inside, a central living room connected to a kitchen/dining area, while two corridors snaked off in opposite directions toward bedrooms. Raymond's daughters stood stiff and waiting, as if summoned to a military tribunal.

"Isabel, Amanda," Raymond said. "You remember Grant."

"Hi, Grant," they replied in unison.

"He'll be staying in the guest room." Raymond pointed down one hallway.

The girls flashed pained smiles and blinked, revealing matching light blue eye shadow. They retreated through sliding doors out to the deck.

Raymond showed Grant to his room. "Don't mind them," he said. "If I didn't have a beach house, they'd be with their mother this weekend." Raymond sighed. "I'm off to dinner with Sandra. Sandwiches and salad are in the fridge. Make yourself at home."

The girls soon clomped out on dates, Isabel wearing platforms, Amanda in pumps.

Grant watched a *Mission: Impossible* rerun as he rifled through record crates by the stereo. Uncle Raymond was near fifty, but he listened to rock, dressed in faded jeans and Earth shoes, and plastered his living room with posters: Nixon naked except for a Watergate Hotel towel around his waist, a "Keep on Truckin'" cartoon image, The Eagles, bearded and glowering, and Linda Ronstadt smiling in concert.

After reading three chapters of *Cat's Cradle*, Grant fell asleep. He woke hearing Raymond strumming an out-of-tune guitar. "I didn't know you played," Grant said, joining him in the morning-lit living room.

"The girls biked to town, so it's safe." Raymond muted his guitar. "Your mother called to say they were too busy to have dinner tonight or lunch tomorrow. But they'll see you Monday, on the drive home."

"Oh..."

"Any plans today, Grant?"

"Check out the beach, maybe swim."

Raymond squinted at the window. "The ocean looks calm, but don't swim alone, okay? The neighbor kids are friendly enough." He began singing in a rumbling voice.

Around 11:30, Grant descended the gray wooden stairway through the long strands of beach grass and sparse stunted trees. He wore a short-sleeved, button-down shirt over Hawaiian trunks that hung to his knees. In a small knapsack, he crammed his Kurt Vonnegut paperback, a cap, some cassette tapes, Coppertone lotion, and a Saran-wrapped ham and Kraft cheese sandwich. He was good for the day.

Grant only traveled two hundred yards before encountering three boys bunched by the surf. The biggest was maybe fourteen, the others about twelve.

The tall one turned. "Who are you? Where you from?"

"Grant." He pointed behind. "Visiting my uncle."

That seemed to relax the boy. "I'm Kevin. Look what we found." A dead fish, over two feet long, lay on its side among wet purple kelp, one large round eye gazing at them. "It's a sea bass." Kevin poked at it with a stick. "I told George and Marcus we're going to gut it. Maybe find something valuable inside."

The air smelled of rank seaweed, low tide, and sunbaked decaying things.

Kevin pulled a serrated knife from a vinyl bag. "Marcus?"

Marcus shook his head.

"George?"

George appeared nauseous.

"Cowards." Kevin slid the fish over to a foot-high sand cliff carved out by the night tide, then sitting, sliced into the fish's belly, allowing the viscous guts to spill out over his hands and onto the beach. They were soon haloed by flies.

George bent over and vomited.

Marcus looked away and so did Grant—avoiding the Domino Effect.

"You want to hang around with us?" Kevin brandished the oozing fish by its tail. "Then help out."

"That's okay."

Kevin offered Grant his knife. "Dig deeper to see if it swallowed any coins."

Grant froze. If he refused, they would shun him, the weekend stretching to eternity as he sulked by Raymond's stairway.

"Come on," Marcus said, "you have to."

"Take the knife," Kevin said to Grant. "What are you, chicken?"

She arrived with quiet precision, padding over on sandals. A little bit older, probably fourteen, Grant thought. A white button-down shirt tied above the waist exposed her belly button, while the faded blue jean shorts below were cut ragged. The teenager moved with confidence in-between the boys and stared at Grant. "Come with me." She walked west.

Grant looked at Kevin's anxious face, the grotesque fish, and then the girl's retreating figure. He followed.

"Where you going?" Kevin said. "Stay away from her. She's wicked weird."

Grant ignored Kevin's words as he caught up with her stride.

"Those guys are stupid," she said. "You don't belong with them." She stopped abruptly to drink in Grant's features. "Wait, how old are you? What's your name?"

"Grant." He felt his mouth twist. The gig was up. "Thirteen." His cheeks burned.

"Oh," she said, "I thought you were much older, like thirteen-and-a-half, or close to fourteen." She had dirty blonde hair, the front chin-length and gusting about her face, the rest tied in braids descending her back.

"I guess I'm heading toward fourteen," Grant replied. When she smiled he felt better. She didn't act like girls in his grade, calling Grant stupid or mocking him. "What's your name?"

"Analisa," she replied. "Can I look through your knapsack?" She had already slipped it off his shoulder.

"Anna or Lisa?"

"Neither, silly. Both." She laughed, but it wasn't jeering, more of an isn't-everything-funny-and-strange laugh. "Keep up with me." Analisa strolled on the soft damp sand as she examined his possessions. The foamy slap of waves wet their feet before sounding a carbonated fizz of retreat. Seagulls shrieked, circling above, while piping plovers and willets pecked along the shoreline for food.

"Walk like we're friends." She gripped his shirt-sleeve, pulled him toward her, then let go, using both hands to rummage through his knapsack.

Up close, Analisa smelled of sun-warmed skin, sea salt, coconut tanning lotion, and unwashed hair.

"*Cat's Cradle*. Is this a good book, Grant?"

"I think it is."

"My mother read his *Breakfast of Champions* book but wouldn't let me see it because of the dirty pictures. So I snuck in her room when she was out and looked."

"Were there?"

"Yup. Drawings of pubic hair and you know, body parts." She stopped, the surf frothing her ankles.

She gave him a sidelong glance. "You've taken biology, right?"

"Yeah, sure," Grant lied. Sex-ed would be taught during fall by Sheldon Roller, PE coach and sometime science teacher. A bear of a man with a crewcut. He advised the boys during recess, "Your most important investment in life is a supporter—your jockstrap. Forget underwear. No protection."

"Look what I brought." Analisa removed a fire engine red, plastic Panasonic tape player with a black wristband from her carry bag. She moved to the dry sand and plunked down on her haunches, crossing her legs.

Grant followed and crouched, neither sitting nor standing.

She reviewed his cassettes. "Grand Funk? No. Led Zeppelin? They're cool. Bad Company? Nah. Fleetwood Mac? Pretty good. KISS?" She paused. "Can I bury this one and we'll both forget you ever had it?"

"Okay."

"No, it's not okay, Grant," Analisa said. "Stick up for what you like." She returned his knapsack and lifted a cassette from her own bag. "Do you know *Tea for the Tillerman*?"

"Cat Stevens."

"You think he's for girls, right?"

"No, my cousins like him. They're guys."

"Sit here." She tapped the sand by her side. "You look really awkward."

He collapsed and scooted over.

"This one's my favorite." Analisa pressed the play button and acoustic guitar sounded, followed by Cat Steven's velvety rasp. She unfurled her towel and lay back, then started singing along. "Longer boats are coming..."

The song seemed to capture the moment, the rhythm matching the lapping waves, coastal noises on the tape blending with avian cries overhead. Grant sat bunched up, gripping his knees. Staring northwest beyond the kids lolling in the shallows, he watched the lazy procession of one ferry approaching Nantucket Harbor while another departed.

Grant angled his neck to peer down at Analisa. He could see through her white shirt to the crocheted blue bikini-top underneath. She wasn't top-heavy like Debbie Steinberg from his class, who seemed to have sprouted enormous breasts overnight.

"What are you doing?" She slid the mirrored sunglasses down her nose.

"Nothing, I was listening."

Analisa burst out laughing and kicked sand at him. She pulled off her shirt, slid out of her cut-offs, and flipped over on her stomach. "Can you rub some lotion on my back? It's in the bag."

Grant squirted the cool cream onto her warm skin and she flinched. He lightly massaged her shoulders.

"I'm not that delicate," she said. "Rub harder."

Grant did, gazing down at the wonder of her tanned back, only broken by the thin straps.

"You're not going to do anything weird, are you?"

"What?"

"You know, try to steal my top, so I have to chase you to get it?"

"No," he said. "Has that happened to you?"

Analisa didn't reply but lay her head on its side. "You seem different." The visible slice of her forehead was furrowed with thought. "Some things are okay if I asked, but not here with people around."

Grant suddenly felt self-conscious straddled above her. He sat on the sand two feet away, facing out toward the swell of the sea as families trudged by. Bickering parents carried beach umbrellas and baskets as children of various sizes trailed after, shadowed beneath drooping hats. The afternoon sun made everything drowsy under its bleaching glare, the day itself slouching to a halt from heat exhaustion. Even gulls had given up flying to watch the dapple of light on waves from the shoreline.

"Where do you live, Analisa?"

She propped herself up on her elbows and pointed east. "Toward Jetties Beach, in a dingy old house with a screened-in porch. It's embarrassing."

Grant nodded.

"We should keep walking." Analisa scooped up a handful of sand and let the grains slip through her fingers. "This is all we have left of summer."

She stared at Grant, and he basked under her green-eyed gaze—neither worshipful nor judgmental, but accepting. He lived in splendor for that prolonged instant, and imagined her radiating glow finally burning off the fog of a lingering childhood.

Analisa buttoned the white shirt that draped down to her thighs, pressed her shorts into the carry bag, and stood. "You take the tape player." She led him further eastward, only pausing to watch an old man fishing from the shore. His face as weathered and pitted as the pilings on the harbor docks.

"Catch anything?" Analisa asked him.

"A small bluefish." The old man frowned. "A striped bass broke my line." His eyes goggled at Analisa's long legs, then he turned back to concentrate on the sea.

"Let's go to the point and watch the ferries coming in," Analisa told Grant. "We'll have a picnic. Did you bring any food?"

"You know I did."

She punched his shoulder gently. "We can split your sandwich."

They slogged onward beneath the dazzle of mid-afternoon sunlight, veering toward the damper sand where the tread was easier. Grant walked ahead.

"Look out." Analisa pulled him back against her. "Horseshoe crab." A spiny tail protruded upwards where the prehistoric-looking crab had buried itself. "Step on one and it'll puncture your foot."

Grant felt her body pressed to his, the warmth of her embrace, and a quivery electric spark tickled through him. He pulled away. "Thanks." Grant thought a moment. "Do you stay out here, year round?"

"No, I just come for the summer." She gestured toward Hyannis or Cape Cod or the continent itself. They continued moving, stepping over driftwood and sand-dusted towels.

"Hey, watch it," a girl of perhaps sixteen yelled. "We're in the middle of a game." A group of bronzed girls in matching red bathing suits played volleyball, their court apparently extending to the shoreline.

Grant and Analisa detoured knee-deep into the water. Varsity status and trophy cups had given these players the hard, arrogant faces of grownups. Their last weekend of summer and they sure as hell were going to enjoy every single moment of fun they were entitled to.

"Ow." Analisa's face contorted. "A jellyfish stung me."

Grant led her ashore. A red welt rose on her shin. He noticed her eyes watering, but she pulled up a shirt tail and wiped them dry.

"I'm not like most girls," she said. "I don't cry, but shit, that really stings."

They had reached a deserted area between Dionis Beach and Jetties Beach where the joyous screams of children and scolding voices of parents receded behind them. Scalloped cirrus clouds formed a canopy above, as if the land and sea had conspired with the sky to cool the sun's glare.

Grant brought Analisa, her arm anchored around his shoulder, toward two abandoned beach chairs. Their aluminum frames showed rust and the crosshatched fabric looked frayed. While she sat massaging her shin, Grant divided the sandwich using his Swiss Army Knife. He handed her the larger half. The ham tasted warm and moist, the cheese bland, and the Wonder Bread had hardened, but it was the best thing he ever ate.

Grant studied the beach around them. He saw black skate shells washed ashore, brittle husks waiting to be wave-battered then pummeled into dried bits to pepper the salt-glazed sand. Long tangles of shiny greenish kelp extended like intestines of leviathans from the deep. Purple-black seaweed embraced a dented buoy, next to cracked clam shells, discarded bottles, starfish—presumably dead—blue soft glass, and dozens of sea-smoothed stones. One of which Analisa examined.

"Do you think these came from outer space? Like pieces of meteors?"

"I don't know," Grant replied. "But that sounds cool."

"Not too much further." She lifted Grant from the low-slung chair.

"Did we pass your house yet?"

"Ages ago. I told you, it's a mess so we're not going there."

"Just wanted to know where you lived."

"So you could visit me at midnight?" She pinched him.

Two boys, probably fourteen, approached from the east. Grant tried to steer Analisa around them, but they shifted to meet head on.

The bigger guy walked straight up to Analisa. "Is that your boyfriend? Or just for today?"

"He's my friend," she said. "As if it's any business of yours."

"I liked you in June. Remember? You split."

"I don't remember you—at all."

"Because you're a tease, a bitch."

"Don't call her that," Grant said.

"Says who?" the burly guy replied. "What are you, twelve?"

Behind him, the smaller boy dangled a horseshoe crab by the tail, then slammed its shell down on the hard sand.

"I think you should show us your boobs," the big guy said to Analisa, leering.

"Yeah," added his friend.

"You owe me." The leader tugged at her shirt collar.

Grant bent his head down and rushed forward, ramming the guy in the stomach.

"You little bastard." He doubled over, gasping. Straightening himself, he punched Grant in the jaw and again just above the eye. The second blow knocked Grant on his back. He got up dizzy, but crouched, preparing to charge again.

"Are you crazy?" The big guy held his belly. "I'll kick your ass, and she's not even worth it." He edged closer, his hands bunched into fists.

Analisa snuck up behind. She swung the Panasonic player, striking the back of the boy's head, and he staggered for an instant. Grant kicked his shin, hobbling him, before Analisa cracked the tape player hard against his skull. The guy stumbled and fell sideways into the shallows, gripping his head. Using both hands, he pushed himself to his knees, his face monstrous with pain.

"We're going to kill both of you..." he started to say, then saw his friend sprinting west along the shoreline, "tomorrow."

Analisa took Grant's arm to run east until they both crumpled onto the sand exhausted. She laughed in gasps and pressed her cheek against his sore jaw.

"I'm sorry I couldn't protect you."

"You tried," she said. "Besides, he was older." The damaged tape player dangled in her grip. Analisa opened it and sighed. "I ruined my Cat Stevens cassette." She extracted it, the tape unspooling and tangled. "But we showed that bully."

"I can buy you a new tape tomorrow."

She stared off at the horizon. "Yeah... tomorrow."

"What time is it?"

"Nearly six," she said. "Let's rest before heading home."

Grant was too dazed to argue.

Analisa unrolled the beach towel in the dunes so they could lay down out of sight. She removed her shirt to use as a blanket when they snuggled together. "I didn't think it would be you today."

"What?"

"Do you want to touch them?"

"Huh?"

She placed Grant's right hand on her left breast.

He squeezed it.

"Ow. Softer." Analisa slid her fingers under his shirt to delicately stroke his chest. "Like that."

He obeyed until she twitched and said, "Stop."

"Was that wrong?"

"No, we'll kiss later." Analisa hugged him, her breathing warm and heavy. Wind buffeted the sand dunes, the long beach grass hissing at the assault then whispering as the air calmed.

Grant realized Analisa had fallen asleep, so he shut his eyes too.

He woke to darkness, the last embers of sunset dying to the west. Grant shivered. He squinted in every direction, but Analisa and her towel were gone. Only the broken Panasonic lodged in the sand convinced him the day hadn't been a dream. The beacon from Brant Point Lighthouse arced through the darkness. Colored lights drifted away from the harbor—a retreating ferry—but it signified nothing. Grant stood, shook his head to clear his thoughts, and followed the lit-up beach house windows back east.

Uncle Raymond waited with a flashlight at the foot of his steps. "Jesus Christ, I thought you drowned." They mounted the wooden stairway into an explosion of light inside. "Where the hell were you?" Raymond asked, his expression a blend of anger and concern. "It's almost nine. Your face, what happened?"

"I met a girl."

Raymond's daughters peeked out from the hallway and giggled.

"And she hit you?"

"No, I was protecting her from an older boy."

Raymond nodded, the redness draining from his complexion. "That's wild," he said, half-smiling. "I'll get some ice. Let's hope the swelling goes away by Monday so your folks don't freak out."

"You're not going to tell them?"

"Hell, no," he said. "No one's going to." Raymond eyed his daughters. "Right?"

They stamped back to their room.

After dinner and after watching *The Rockford Files*, Grant nodded off listening to the concussion of waves against the shore.

On Sunday morning, Grant put on a tennis hat to hide his bruise and tramped down the beach searching. Girls sprouted everywhere, but not Analisa. He finally found the weather-beaten house with a long screened-in porch up on a bluff. Climbing through dunes, Grant pressed his face against the screen. It smelled like ointment and powdery perfume, of dust and dryness, of elderly people. A bloated cat lazed on a rocking chair.

"Hello!" He rapped his knuckles against the wood of the screen door until a woman older than his grandmother shuffled over in a bathrobe and slippers.

"What is it?" She squeaked the door open. "Are you the paper boy?"

"No, is your, uh, granddaughter here, Analisa?"

"Analisa?" she said. "There haven't been children in this house for thirty years. Go play somewhere else." She slapped the door shut.

Grant tried the neighboring houses without luck, a jagged panic lancing his stomach. He meandered along the beach before encountering familiar faces.

"Did your girlfriend ditch you?" Kevin asked.

"No," Grant said, "I can't find her. Just wondered which house she lived in?"

Kevin stopped tossing the Frisbee to his friends. "That girl doesn't live here. She takes the ferry from Hyannis on weekends, causes trouble for a day, then goes home." He gave Grant an incredulous look. "I tried to warn you. Most locals know to stay away." He twirled the orange Frisbee on one finger. "I doubt she'll come back this weekend. Maybe next June." The boy who disemboweled a fish acted almost tender. "She leads guys on then disappears. They wander around dazed for the rest of the summer. So you got lucky." His mouth tightened. "Because summer's over tomorrow."

Grant spent much of Sunday languishing on the planks of a jetty, watching ancient fishermen cast their lines as the ferries came and went. Only thirteen and he already felt old and discarded like the busted Panasonic tape player. Grant returned to Raymond's at four and they walked the cobblestone streets of town where he purchased a copy of *Tea for the Tillerman.*

Grant listened to Cat Stevens through that fall and following spring, but eventually forgot about the album, forgot about Analisa for over forty years.

Then one night in Whole Foods, as he waited at the brightly-lit beer and wine bar while his wife bought gluten-free zucchini bread, "Longer Boats" played on their system. The entire weekend came rushing back to him. But Uncle Raymond was dead now, home prices on Nantucket were even higher than in the Hamptons, Cat Stevens had become Yusef Islam, and no one like Jimmy Carter would ever be president again.

Grant closed his eyes to summon a final memory. Before they fell asleep together that beach Saturday in the shadows of late afternoon, Analisa had pointed toward a sluggish, confused house fly. "If you could live for just one day, Grant, would this be that day?"

"Maybe, I guess. I don't know."

She gripped his wrist. "It would be for me..."

Grant opened his eyes.

A woman of similar vintage seated nearby at the Whole Foods bar looked over, her face sympathetic. "This song always gets to me too." She handed him a napkin, smiled, then turned back to drink her red wine.

SHIPWRECKED ON SHIPROCK

Driving US-64 west along the ragged collarbone of New Mexico, leaving the Farmington of young men hauling shit in their trucks, of unrepentant Trump voters, and jug-eared rodeo cowboy seniors receding in your rear view mirror. Ahead is the Navajo Nation and Shiprock— a somewhat destitute and forlorn place. On the glide path approaching Four Corners, a dislocation of boundaries occurs as the separate states merge into one vast desert country. Watch the surreal mushroom landscapes mash up against the unsightly aluminum-sided, drywall manifestations of humankind. To visit is to seek out some primordial, seeming eternal magnificence; to live here is to obviate one's surroundings, ignore them, and thrive despite them.

From inside a rented Nissan, a ghost blue haze is visible draped over the far off mountain range that seems otherworldly, like an alien planet projection. In the near distance, the gargantuan Shiprock rises jagged and monolithic. Omnipresent when studied, until it blends in with the sky and clouds over time. Town mascot or just another hallucinatory upthrust? For you, a compass: *Am*

I approaching it or is it receding behind me? And if I'm passing below it, must have taken a goddamn wrong turn at the junction. Old New Mexico route signs once colored tree bark brown or black on white are pummeled and faded, even knocked down, so best to engage an inner radar.

You question Robinson riding shotgun whether you should keep going?

His attire: a flannel shirt, khaki shorts, and sandals, large forehead gleaming. As usual, he is telepathic. "Yes to everything," he says before you can ask, followed by a single "ha!" Robinson is a legendary recording engineer who never leaves his studio. Untethered for this trip.

The thirty odd miles between Farmington and Shiprock are speckled with white and Day-Glo orange placards. *Safety Corridor – Double Fines for Speeding*, watch your speedometer, check your side mirrors, and *Road Work Ahead – Next 50 Miles*. Single story businesses line the roadsides: tire repair, self car wash, pawn shop, Navajo fry bread, 7-Eleven, church bingo, Dollar Tree, rodeo billboards, old pump gas stations named Alon, Mustang, and Giant. Women's faces framed in laundromat windows show unguarded expressions. Boredom. Resignation. Fatigue.

Extended wagons hitched to pickup trucks veer across lane dividers, nearing banged-up, rust-bucket vehicles that gush charcoal clouds from exhaust pipes while silvery horse trailers reflecting sunlight come on all rattle and thrum as they jostle over the asphalt.

Hitchhiking, fallen into obscurity and disrepute in much of America, remains a method of travel in the Southwest among Native Americans. Though some here prefer the term American Indian. From every cross street, dusty dirt and white sand blow then whirlwind into the air. Young hitchhikers stand immersed in personal cyclones, bandannas pulled down like masked bandits. Amid the blurry static of particles they resemble Bedouin nomads in a desert sandstorm. When traffic staggers to a crawl, the Nissan slows down for one guy.

"Going south to Window Rock at the junction?" he asks you, not seeing Robinson.

"No, heading west, all the way to Arizona."

So Bandanna waves you on. And after you edge back into the traffic flow of 64, he remains waiting for a ride, buffeted by the elements as if that was normal, while you barely survived twenty seconds of the opened car window allowing a hot gritty blast of Southwest reality to scour your pale-assed, sensitive face.

You drove out to this nuclear blasted openness for inspiration, for rejuvenation, and you speed like a motherfucker because the distances are vast and the towns sparse beyond Shiprock and all the way across the state border. Practically flying. But the faster one drives, the wider the desert spreads to slow any sense of forward motion. It's important to know how far to go, and exactly how long to stay so you can return bearing gifts of revelation, the hypnagogic visions left over from our Earth ancestors. Stay too long and dry up into a desiccated husk, parched and aged before your time, the social rot and soul pollution you sought to escape, a fool's errand in the grizzled face of dehydration. Go too far and you'll haunt the horizon as a heat wave mirage—*what the hell is that?*—to be eye-rubbed away by weary travelers in disbelief.

"Should I turn back?" you ask the passenger seat.

"I ain't scared," Robinson replies and cackles. "Further in; further out."

What does he have left to lose?

The whole world, the tufted crust of the planet, is laid out ahead. *Rough road. Watch your speed.* Beyond the flat top mesa stretching for miles, past two looming buttes and through the conical hoodoos hugging the route you hope to find...sanctuary. Peace. Closure.

Welcome to Arizona.

The tribal elders, and the young badasses—who could give a damn about spirits or traditions—and the uranium cowboys all know you. They've seen your kind coming for years, decades, from deep into the previous century, clutching Kerouac and Edward Abbey paperbacks. Seeking something; escaping everything. Though not every astronaut who blasts off into space truly returns. Some come back as shells, stamping around on the minimal battery power of life, rendered aimless and broken.

And the locals are right. *Desert Solitaire* is mashed in your bag along with *Desolation Angels*, because Kerouac describes his fire lookout duty on Desolation Peak in the Cascades of Washington State. That's the link. Edward Abbey was a fire lookout at the North Rim of the Grand Canyon, blurred and distorted in his novel *Black Sun*. Not random travel books; everything brought along has a purpose.

Foolish outlanders perish in the desert terrain between May and September, hiking in hundred degree heart attack heat, running out of food and water, or drowned anonymous by a flash flood in a remote canyon. *Remember running from a muddy river of rain at the base of the slot canyon that bisects Tent Rocks?* Upon reaching open air, the hail hammered down until that prized fedora was mashed and shapeless, your neck pimpled red from the stinging downfall.

So when the aged indigenous man—who doesn't hate you but finds you a bit pathetic—at a no name gas station advises, "Better fill up your tank here," you damn straight listen. Because you're thirty miles away from the sign that will tell you what tumbleweed town you're thirty miles away from. Mexican Water, Bluff, Rock Point?

Continue on, past indifferent horses grazing at the lip of the road, beyond fenced ranch spreads, until the only visible motion is the oil pumpjacks see-sawing back and forth like grotesque outdoor iron sculptures. Not a soul in sight.

Slow down. Cattle crossing, reads the sign.

"That don't not make sense." Imagine Robinson smiling, all teeth and burly beard. "Indubitably." You've memorized your friend's expressions. They linger on this journey.

Time melts and stretches like the freight train snaking through the hills and flats in the distance, spread out so long you can't see the locomotive or the caboose. It staggers and clanks along at five, maybe ten mph, heading west to some far-off destination. Will the people waiting still be alive when the train arrives? And if so, will they even remember the freight they once ordered?

"I should write a song for the lizards and rattlers that thrive out here."

"Hell yeah." Robinson fades, leaving you alone for the duration.

Families bury the mortal remains, but friends decide how to inter and consecrate their friendship. Plant his ghost somewhere righteous along the route before moving on. Leave the wadded-up grief behind.

Again the vast space overwhelms and dominates thought. Can one comprehend the people, and this land once the base of an ocean, or the substrata of matter: Precambrian, greenstone, granitic rock, and Navajo sandstone colored red, yellow, black or green by iron minerals? No. Logic is a slim twig to hang one's hat on. Life maybe gives you five or ten more trips to such a place. Make them count.

Tourists visiting canyon country freak over the massive silence. Humanity lives among constant sound: beeps, pings, people shouting into phones, drones buzzing overhead, car alarms, ambulance sirens, jets, helicopters, motorcycles revving, e-bikes, refrigerators, arguing neighbors. At some point the roar becomes normal, white noise, a sign of civilization. Stripped of such distraction, one is naked, alone with their own interior voices.

I could have spent more time with him this last year. His last year. I didn't call because the fucker never answered his phone. Why didn't I join him for that Grant-Lee Phillips concert he invited me to six months ago? I figured there would be another one and another one after...

You persist in writhing amid the serpentine coils of *what if.* How many hikes will it take to dispel the guilt gas? Bring water, maps, and more water if you leave the car. The destination is ambiguous, perhaps nonexistent; the journey itself remains the essential fluid truth.

Like photography, existing on the Colorado Plateau is all about timing: early mornings and the hour before sunset. If you think you've found heaven at Four Corners, remember that conditions are half past hell. Admire it, even reach for it, but if you can't turn away and retreat, or don't understand holding your breath in a slow motion explosion, then you risk dry drowning in the desert. The coyotes' atonal yowls will mark the moment and the place where you dropped, synapses shorting out like the electrical system in a car.

"Cause of death?" Those who care may ask.

"He blew his fuse box."

WALKING MAN

Todd Marcus crouched down in the man-made greenbelt of chaparral separating his housing tract from a neighboring one in Agoura Hills. The previous hours of walking, running, and scrambling had left him smelling like a wild animal. He hiked up the manufactured hillside seeking a vantage point to spot his wife's Escalade once she turned off Highway 101 and approached their house. Barbara alone could make today's nightmare go away. Then it might be safely tucked into memory and only brought up after it achieved a humorous status when discussed over a boozy dinner among friends.

Todd had been driving Moorpark Road toward Whole Foods in Thousand Oaks when his GMC Yukon started making weird noises, the engine stuttering. Damn, he thought, the whole point of buying a $60,000 car was to avoid mechanical problems.

"Get a Toyota or a Honda," Barb had told him. "They never break down."

But he wanted something bigger, more expensive, and powerful-looking. He was forty-nine and deserved it. Hell, you could cook Porterhouse steaks on the Yukon's massive grill.

The SUV hiccupped and slowed as he entered the shopping plaza. Todd coasted to a space at the far edge of the Whole Foods parking area where the engine died. Jumping out, he popped the hood and stared in confusion. He knew nothing about cars, beyond that they cost a fuck-ton to fix.

Late September winds in Southern California blew hot and near cyclonic. As Todd moved around the front bumper, a sudden gust slammed the driver side door closed. The event didn't trouble Todd until he heard the auto-lock feature click every door in the vehicle shut. Then came the realization that he'd left the keys in the ignition, as well as leaving the stupid fanny pack his wife bought him holding his wallet and iPhone inside. He cursed himself before remembering the little pay-as-you-go cell phone buried within his pocket for emergencies. Better yet, Triple A sat just on the other side of Wilbur Road, a mere hundred yards away.

Todd set off through the parking lot and past the Arco gas station, then hustled across Wilbur to Triple A's entrance. Closing time five p.m. His crap phone didn't have a clock, but he figured it to be just after five. He banged on the door until a tall black man in a shirt and tie showed up to shake his head, point at his watch, and signal toward the daily hours sign on the glass door.

"But I broke down," Todd yelled.

The man held his hands out with a wistful expression before moving away.

Todd called their 800 roadside assistance number.

"Yes sir, and your card number please?" the operator asked.

Todd not only didn't have his card, but he hadn't renewed this year. "Uh, my wife's card will cover me."

"Yes," the woman said, her voice sounding Midwestern flat and a thousand miles off. "Have her call us, give her number, then we can send a tow truck."

"This is an emergency," Todd said, though it really wasn't. "Let me speak to your supervisor." He got transferred to a limbo of smooth jazz immersed in fuzzy static.

"Edward Dayton here," a man finally said. "I understand you don't have our card but your wife does. Company rules are that she must call this in."

"But I—"

"Sir, do you need a tow truck or did you lock your keys in your car?"

"Possibly, but yes, my keys are inside."

The supervisor lowered his voice. "You might want to try a coat hanger through the window, or contact your wife. Thanks for reaching out to the Triple A hotline." The call ended.

Todd smiled, remembering that he kept the Yukon's driver side window cracked. *Just need a hanger*, he thought.

Through an alleyway, behind the office, Todd found a large green dumpster the adjoining businesses shared. Opening the lid, he nearly gagged from the rotting food stench. Broken pieces of wood, plastic, and cardboard sheets sat bunched together, while discarded clothing lay near the bottom. He caught a glint of metal, a shirt drooping off a hanger. Unfortunately, it was impossible to reach. Todd looked over his shoulder as traffic whizzed past on Wilbur Road, but being 5:30 on a Friday, no one lingered in a private business parking area.

Todd clambered up to the dumpster's edge. If he held onto the rim and leaned his upper-torso down, he could grab the shirt with his free hand and extricate it. Easy. Todd would wash and disinfect his hands later at home, and send his pressed pants to the dry cleaners tomorrow. He hung over the lip, face descending as he tried not to inhale the ancient stink rising from the dumpster's stomach. Stretching, he gripped the shirt and pulled, but it caught fast on something. Todd tumbled head first into the dumpster, landing amid the soiled food and three inches of dirty rainwater pooled at the bottom. Disgusted, he pried the hanger loose and climbed over slats of plywood back out.

Todd's light blue, button-down shirt from Nordstrom's had brown stains on it. His slacks showed dirt marks and wet spots, including at the crotch, and he hand-combed pieces of eggshells and orange rinds out of his hair. "Shit, fuck, shit." But Todd had secured the hanger and felt victorious while dodging the cross-traffic on Wilbur to reach his Yukon.

He worked the curved end of the hanger through the space in his window, then fished at the door lock. The first attempts failed, so he bent the curve into a tighter loop for better gripping power. As Todd jiggled the taut wire, the car alarm went off. No one paid any attention to them, so he continued his efforts until a small utility truck came speeding over.

"Step away from the vehicle," an older man shouted.

"What the hell do you think you're doing?" He screeched to a halt.

Though Todd and his wife Barbara had only lived in Agoura Hills and shopped in Thousand Oaks for three months, he'd never witnessed a Four Seasons Center Security truck before. Todd ignored him, because these guards had no guns or real authority, but he noticed the man speaking into a walkie talkie of a phone.

Todd felt bad for the old fart, probably seventy-five. Shouldn't be working in California's September heat, but back at home binge-watching C-SPAN, or whatever PBS nature shows seniors watched. "This is my car." Todd approached him. "I locked myself out. Just trying to open the door and get my wallet and keys."

"You own a car like that?" The grizzled man studied Todd.

"Yes, I own it." Todd realized he looked a mess, hair disheveled, brow sweaty, clothes stained, and a vague fecal aroma perfuming him from plunging into garbage. "See I was in a dumpster across the street and—"

"A dumpster diver." The security guard shook his head. "That's not allowed here at Four Seasons Center," he said, as if the self-appointed mayor of the parking lot. "Just tell the police when they arrive. Wish we could turn off that damn alarm."

"I don't have my keys." Todd tried to remain calm. Whether it was the heat, the wind, or the geezer guard pressing his mottled, sunburned face up close, Todd panicked. He ran across West Moorpark Road looking for a place to sit down and call his wife.

Inside Peet's Coffee, he tried Barbara twice; both times her voicemail picked up. He detailed his location and asked her to come get him. After ten minutes passed, Todd realized he'd never contacted her with his pay-as-you-go phone before. Undoubtedly, she saw the unfamiliar number, figured it was telemarketer spam and ignored it. He sighed, then texted Barbara. For whatever reason, a "message undelivered" balloon appeared. *Piece of crap phone.* Todd only had a few friends locally and their numbers were stored on his iPhone, not in his memory.

Todd summoned Barb's last words before they each drove separately from Agoura to Thousand Oaks. "I'm stocking up at Trader Joe's," she had said, "then The Oaks Mall, farmer's market, and getting my roots done at Hair Palace."

"I need to measure desks at Office Depot, get us dinner, and pay our Macy's bill," he said.

"If the timing works out," Barbara said, "we can meet at sevenish at Sunland Winery Tasting Room. Otherwise, dinner at home by eight."

None of her stops were a short distance from Peet's, but Todd could reach The Oaks in ten minutes. He soon realized that no one walked on Moorpark Road; it was too hot for even the craziest joggers. Latino families bunched up inside minivans and rusted station wagons stared at him with sadness, while rich white people encased in their gleaming outsized vehicles either ignored Todd or studied him with grim expressions.

He felt naked, totally exposed. Todd's environment was no longer temperature-controlled or wind-shielded. His sunglasses lay broken at the bottom of the rank dumpster.

Of course nobody strolled the streets. Thousand Oaks was a prefabricated city, built of housing communities, malls, shopping centers, and industrial parks. No "old town" existed, nor a Main Street. Anglo history didn't stretch back much beyond the town's incorporation in 1964. Chumash Indians once occupied this land, then the Spanish, and now big box stores.

In the distance, Todd spotted two police cars cruising the opposite side of Moorpark, heading for Whole Foods. He turned north on Brazil Street, which intersected with the curve of Wilbur Road. Minutes later, he hiked the rise and decline of Hillcrest Drive feeling winded. Damn, he used to run two or three miles a night. Again Todd found himself alone, the sidewalks apparently only ornamental. Behind and across the boulevard, he noticed a police car pull into the mall's entrance, so he continued speed-walking along Hillcrest toward the farmer's market.

He checked his phone. No texts, no calls. Distracted, he almost bumped into a man wheeling a grocery cart. "Sorry." Todd lurched out of the way.

"You need one of these for your stuff." The stranger motioned his head toward his cart. "You also got to stay off major roads. Travel the parking lots and back streets."

"No, you're mistaken," Todd said, realizing the man was homeless. "I'm not like you..." He stopped himself.

"Cause you're white? You're a walking man in Thousand Oaks, so you are like me." The man gazed over Todd's shoulder and flinched. "Cops driving out of the mall. Come on, we can hide by that medical center." He rolled his cart right on Marin Street, then scuttled inside a tree-shrouded lot.

Todd followed and they both crouched in the sliver of bushes and grass that separated the parking lot from Hillcrest—invisible to the medical center and the Drive.

"I'm Deon," the man said, "and you're new in town. Need a blanket to sleep on later?"

"No, thanks."

"Stay hidden until it gets dark, then hit the dumpsters after midnight. Whole Foods throws away some quality shit. Chicken breasts, fish."

The police car slowed and idled by the corner of Hillcrest and Marin, less than twenty feet away. "Alleged person of interest seen traveling in this direction," one officer said.

"Possibly the suspect trying to break into a car before," his partner replied.

"Security guard said that guy was a dumpster diver. Acted squirrely, maybe off his meds."

"Seen walking across Thousand Oaks. What the hell? No one does that. Alzheimer's?"

"The guard claimed he looked late-forties, fiftyish. Pretty early for dementia, but he might have escaped a treatment center."

"Residents complained too," the second cop said. "They don't even like running into their neighbors outside, much less a deranged man."

Flat on his stomach, Deon edged away from Todd. "For real? You all messed-up? You're not going to hurt me are you?"

"No," Todd said, but Deon soon hurried off, abandoning his grocery cart.

Todd felt an alien sensation. He had never caused fear in another man, especially not an unhoused African

American. He crouched, watching patients dart from cosmetic surgeons' offices with bandaged noses, giant sunglasses over their eyes, or rolls of gauze turbaned around their heads, before ducking into luxury cars.

Todd and Barbara had relocated to Los Angeles and gotten married a few years after 9/11 when New York became unbearable. Then, after L.A. life got complicated, with too much activism and traffic and downtown crime, they retreated to Agoura Hills: a place for people who wanted to live and shop in peace. Beyond the annoyance of wildfires, the Mediterranean climate was superb. A haven from news of immigration caravans, from racial unrest after so many police shootings. Thirty miles outside of Los Angeles in a sunny land of manicured elegance, they didn't have to apologize for being white, nor explain to anyone why they always voted for the candidate who kept their taxes lower, their investment accounts higher. It was accepted, part of the rarefied air local residents paid to breathe.

When Hillcrest Drive appeared safe, Todd loped another block, but the sound of a helicopter descending made him sprint into the next office park. He scurried beneath a stand of oak trees until the wup-wup-wup sound receded and the helicopter rose up to merge with the residual smoky haze from recent wildfires. When he reached the north end of Hillcrest, a rusted, sagging Ford pickup slowed. A middle-aged, Mexican man wearing a baseball cap offered two crumpled dollar bills.

Todd waved him away. *"No es necesario."*

The man pointed at Todd's eyes. *"Ojos de la muerte."* He drove off.

Barbara exited The Oaks, climbed back into her Escalade, then drove toward the farmer's market. She texted, *WTH, Todd?* He hadn't returned her previous calls or texts. Did he sneak off to see the latest stupid Marvel Universe film at Muvico Theaters 14? *Guardians of the Avengers*, or some such shit.

She hoped to make things right over a glass of wine. It always took the edge off a brutal day of shopping and driving in Southern California. Last evening, Barbara abruptly ended their weekly date night sex. She was forty-six and didn't want a surprise pregnancy or the side-effects of taking the pill. Since Todd wouldn't get snipped, Barbara made him wear a condom. After he finished, Todd crawled under the sheets. Sixteen years into their marriage, she didn't need him sputtering around down there.

"It's okay, really, I'm fine," she said. "Can we just watch *Succession*?"

Todd went along, but seemed miffed in the morning, moodier than usual. Maybe that's why he wasn't responding now.

Instead, Barbara kept receiving messages from Amy, one of her book club friends. Ladies in their mid-forties who drank and talked about books, or more often, the movie versions of books they hadn't bothered to read. However, Amy desired a daily friendship, and as a divorced woman perpetually looking for the right man, she had become needy, tedious.

Amy's most recent text read: *Barb, you didn't reply to my last message. And your previous one didn't end with an LOL or an emoji. Feeling confused. Is everything okay?*

Barbara switched the car radio to KVTA news. The temperature at six still hovered in the nineties. She frowned. Even though Barbara existed in the air-conditioned world of her Escalade, of box stores, and in her climate-controlled home, the idea of suffering even a minute of that heat seemed inconceivable.

"It's a warm one out there," Ridge Whitley said. "Any more info about slow-downs on the 101 from the traffic copter, Pete?"

"Just the usual Friday after-work traffic," Pete yelled over the thrum of helicopter rotors. "But there is a lot of chatter about the so-called 'walking man' in Thousand Oaks. Apparently, he has traveled for miles on foot and no one is sure why. Some speculate he might be unstable. Others wonder if he's making an unspecified protest against cars and oil companies."

"That won't go over well in Southern California, Pete," Ridge said. "We love our big cars. By the way, what's your ride?"

"A Toyota Highlander," Pete said. "How about you?"

"I'm a Humvee guy, myself."

"You boys are so macho," Heather piped in. "I'm happy in my little Prius."

"That's right, Heather used to work in the People's Republic of San Francisco." Both men laughed.

"Anyway," Pete said, "police are determining whether the walking man is the guy who attempted to rob a Chase Bank on Monday, or just an eco-protester wandering a little far from L.A."

"That is so wacky," Heather said. "E.T. call home."

Barbara glanced at her phone. Three texts with no message from a 747 number she didn't recognize. Then

Barbara remembered an evening last month. When Todd went to Ventura, she slipped over to the nearby Boar Dough Tasting Room for a single glass of wine. One bottle later she found herself flirting with a rich-looking, fiftyish man. *What was it, Bronson Maybank?* She had no intention of cheating, but Bronson Maybank's name sounded so sexy, like heliports, thousand count bed sheets, and the ultra-rare Amex Black Card, so she gave him her cell number. The failed texts must have come from him. Barbara felt intrigued, but also mildly annoyed Bronson had waited a whole damn month. Now she would make him wait too.

Barbara bought gluten-free bread and organic salad at the farmer's market, then rushed south for her hair appointment.

It was six-thirty when Todd reached the farmer's market. He couldn't find Barb's white Escalade, and the prosperous locals milling about glanced at him with suspicion. Finally, a young saleswoman at the honey table approached. "Hey, you're that guy."

"What?" Todd stared into her eyes.

"I support your Forrest Gump trip." She smiled. "You don't seem crazy, but you're kind of a hot mess. Here take these." She handed him a brown hippie shirt, probably made from hemp, and a wool cap.

"Uh, thanks."

Through the scrim of customers thronged around produce tables, Todd saw a police car pull up fifty yards away. He decided to clear the whole matter up. The two officers spotted him and walked casually in his direction.

However, one cop carried a stun gun while the other unlatched his holster. Did they consider him violent? Todd had never bought into the concept of white privilege, but without his expensive SUV and credit cards, he was nothing. A question mark.

Todd bolted in the opposite direction out of the market's enclosure and climbed a chain link fence, tearing gashes in his pants. Beyond the fence lay an alleyway bordered with a line of white birch trees. He pushed through them and plunged down into an open metal trough where gutters from a warehouse's slanted roof drained into. Instead of water, the trough held a sludge that smelled like excrement. He tramped through it, crossed another alley and finally wedged himself into a hollow space under a hedge used to wall-off a property. The police car drove down the alley, but passed him and disappeared. Todd trembled, waiting for dusk huddled in a fetal position.

At sunset he emerged to see runners huffing and puffing along the sidewalks. He replaced his soiled blue shirt with the hemp one, and pressed the fuzzy hipster cap down over his brow. If he jogged, Todd could blend in and make the five miles back to Agoura Hills in just over an hour. When he tried Barb again, the phone flashed a "no signal" message. Useless. After a mile of loping along the frontage road that paralleled Highway 101, he reached the fluorescent-lit parking area for Sunland Winery.

A college-age kid raced over. "Sorry buddy, we're a private business. This is valet parking and we require a car." His face softened. "But I've got a half-sandwich and some soda."

"No, that's not why I'm here," Todd said. "Did you see a woman in a white Escalade with big, expensive-looking hair?" Todd guessed from the darkening sky it was seven.

"No, I'd remember that." The young guy grinned and relaxed. "Wait, you're the walking man." He slapped Todd on the shoulder. "Bro, I'm totally down with your whole deal. We are raping and destroying Mother Earth. Your protest is so legit."

"What?"

"But listen, dude, those shoes are cringe. They smell like shit—literally." The youth hustled to his booth then came hurrying back. "Take my Crocs, man. I would so leave this job and join you, it's just I have to pay my rent."

Todd hurled his disgusting filth-encrusted shoes into the darkness beyond the lot and slipped into the weird, foot-shaped Crocs. "Thanks." He fist-bumped the valet and continued jogging south.

In an hour, Todd reached Agoura Hills and tried to orient himself in darkness. The damn place was a sea of similar-looking housing tracts, some with dozens of identical homes stretched out in rows. Todd vaguely knew where he lived, but his GMC had plotted the exact destination, telling him how many miles, where to turn, and where to park. Should he take Hillrise Lane to Mountain View Court, or was it Moonrise Lane to Valley View Court? Don't panic. Breathe.

Todd decided to wait on the artificial hill that separated Mountain View from Valley View. Barbara would return by eight. She was very precise about dining and got cranky as hell when her blood sugar level dipped. There had been many vagaries and even outright lies in their sixteen years of marriage, but her word in relation to meal times remained solid. He hunkered down, searching for the familiar blinding HID headlights she custom-installed on her Escalade.

Barbara drove into Sunland Winery around 7:45. She toured the lot but didn't see Todd's black GMC rising above the Mercedes, Jaguars, and Porsches. A cute young valet raced over toward her looking agitated, so she turned to exit, almost side-swiping him. *Damn, I got here late. Todd must have driven home.* Luckily, she'd brought a wine bottle to her hair appointment and had achieved a manageable buzz. She stared at her phone. *Todd must be really pissed, unless... Could he be holding out for a blowjob apology?*

Barbara surged onto 101 heading south, cars honking at her. What, did they expect her to signal every time she changed lanes? The good news was she'd be back at eight as planned. If Todd kept acting like a moody little bitch, he could sleep in a separate bedroom. They had five after all. She veered across three lanes and exited on Cheesebro Road. In a few minutes she approached the entranceway to Mountain View Court and decelerated. Barbara picked up her phone and replied to Bronson Maybank's failed texts. *Is that you? Haven't heard back. Meet again at the same place?*

Todd recognized Barb's high beams weaving along Hollow Brook Road. He descended through the chemise, the ceanothus, and manzanita, but twisted his ankle in a ditch. Limping downward, he tripped, falling flat by the edge of the road. The stupid cell phone launched from his pocket, skittering onto the asphalt. It began to ping. Searing pain shot through Todd's lower leg as he crawled out to retrieve it. *Must read the texts—now.*

Barbara decided to add a more flirtatious follow-up to Bronson. Slowing to thirty-five mph, she concentrated on her iPhone and barely saw the wild animal on all fours crossing the road. Something brown and mangy-looking. According to local news, California wildfires in nearby mountain ranges had displaced a variety of creatures: deer, bears, and even mountain lions. *Oh please, anything but a neighbor's dog.*

In the instant she pressed send on her text and squeezed her eyes shut, Barbara's only thought was, *Shit, I hope Triple A will cover this...*

I'VE GOT MY PROBLEMS

I've lived in this town for years, one of those coastal cities in Southern California, because everything here moves slow. I can be lazy as shit and still stay ahead of the game. Decades kind of blur into each other. Half the people are either retired or not working, so it's easy for a directionless guy like me to fit right in.

Five years ago an ex-girlfriend asked me, "What's your five year plan?" I didn't know then and am still wondering now. I don't relate to the type of question that requires an answer. Yeah, I've got my problems, but friends will tell you I'm solid and dependable. Always there when they're flush, but scarce as hell when they're in trouble. I mean, who needs someone else to remind them, *Wow, you are so fucked*? No one does.

I'm heading home to my little cottage and I spot a good buddy standing outside. Warms the cockles of my heart. We are so tight, despite him being much older and us having nothing in common. Guess I consider him like family, you know, a stepfather or a cousin once removed. I would so love to speak to this ultra-solid dude, except he's my landlord and I get a funny feeling he's waiting there because I'm four weeks late on rent. So I duck into some bushes across the street to meditate and practice deep yoga breathing. It's purely out of consideration though. If he saw me, it would mean bullshitting him with a story that isn't true and then him issuing me an ultimatum. Amigos don't pull that crap on each other. Not cool. Those little things can wear down a friendship. I don't want to lie to this awesome major bro I barely know because that just feels wrong. Better we don't meet and he just wonders. A state of unspoken uncertainty is a much healthier place for us to be in our relationship. And life is really all about the unanswered questions.

Landlord guy finally leaves when the sun goes down and I sneak in through my back window. He's got some paper taped up on the front door but I don't read so well without my glasses. Seriously need a replacement set. Has it been three years already? Time really flies when you're flying blind. Thoughtful of him to attach a padlock to keep away neighborhood thieves. The power's off inside and I'm not sure why. A huge stack of unopened mail sits on my table and the answer might be buried somewhere in there, but I'm not that curious. Instead, I make a quick sandwich which tastes soggy and warm and actually pretty awful. Hard to identify food in my dark fridge anymore. The bread feels really fuzzy and dimensional on my tongue though.

Still, I can sing and play my broken guitar in the darkness until the neighbors complain—and they do—but I also enjoy the arts, you know, watching TV and surfing the Internet. So I wash my face and say, Hallelujah, because the water is running today, then I amble outside to visit one of my girlfriends with Wi-Fi. I don't have a lot of energy when I'm hungry and my stomach is struggling to digest moldy food, so I head for the nearest one: Charlene's place. Char is like the love of my life. Our deal is so fucking magical it's hard to describe to people how we're soul-mates and complete each other. Though it's been complicated ever since she put the restraining order on me and began dating that local cop.

I check the entire block but his car is nowhere in sight, so I study her sitting on the couch awhile through the window before lightly tapping on the door.

"Get the hell out of here, Randy," she says, obviously joking, after she opens up. When you share a deep love, you talk this way. Verbal foreplay. It's like being for real and in the moment.

"Baby," I say, "I just want to check my e-mails and watch a horror flick. You still have Netflix and HBO?"

"Victor will be off work in a half-hour. Do you really want him finding you here after last time?"

I feel the space where a tooth used to live in my mouth, where the wind whistles through on stormy nights, and think maybe she's making sense. I want to tell her she's the girl of my dreams, except I don't dream—ever. Just ten hours of dark fucking black space. "Sure, Char, that's cool. Listen, could I just use your can? I ate something funky before and it's burning through my system like a meteor."

"Are you serious?"

"Fifteen minutes tops." I push past her toward the throne.

I don't know how these tender moments between us always end with Charlene crying, me running, and sirens blaring, but the ways of love are mysterious.

Seven blocks away on Anacapa Street is where Tricia lives. Our bond is special, an unspoken thing that churns deep down inside, sort of the way you feel after a meal at Taco Bell. She has an open house policy so I try the door but it's locked. Chained. Bolted. Weird, man, that must be Tricia's secret signal for me to use the kitchen window, which I do. Once inside, I hear all this loud thumping and groaning. I tip-toe toward the back bedroom to see this tall, overweight guy banging her.

I chuckle to myself and go make a quality sandwich out of ham, turkey, and cheese in the fridge. If you're wondering why I'm not jealous, it's because we're evolved, on a higher plane. We work hard on our open relationship. Neither of us owns each other. Total freedom. The other reason is the big dude—I happened to see his pimpled ass, and will need serious alcohol to remove that memory—is also Tricia's husband. Yeah, life is complicated, but I'm all about simplicity. I can predict from previous experience that they'll be back there for at least another twenty minutes, meaning I have just enough time to check my e-mails.

Jesus fucking Christ! It's bills, complaints, notices, summons, threats. I can't handle this stress so I mark it all as spam. Which makes me hungry—sandwich time. I want good news: sweepstakes prizes I've won but need to collect, some generous stranger from Africa who wants to give me money, horny women in jail desperate to meet me. Guess I'm talking out loud. That shit happens when your hearing goes. No connection to my ten years as a roadie for Metallica.

"Hey, who's there?" the husband shouts from the hallway.

I dash out the door, because I don't want to see a naked dude rushing me. Been there, done that.

"Randy," a righteous friend yells to me from across the street. He's like my brother-in-law from another mother-in-law.

I get a bad vibe and dart around the house through an alleyway. I mean we all need to work in these hard times, but parole officer seems below my good buddy's abilities. We respect each other's life choices, but he finds it hard to separate business from friendship. I do him a solid by bolting. Naturally I'm out of breath, so I find a little water in a bowl on a nearby porch and slurp it down. When some unfortunate barking ensues, I'm sprinting like a Kenyan marathon runner on crystal meth.

Really need a to-do list. Most nights I make some serious distances, so I should score one of those mileage gizmo things people use, for my health and well-being. There's an old girlfriend I remember who would definitely loan me hers. Trouble is she lives in a fancy gated place high in the hills. I won't really have time to ask, using words. More of a get-in, get-out operation. But when I do return it she'll understand I was just borrowing it and be super-grateful. Life has its ups and downs. We lose one superficial possession and gain something more profound—knowledge.

Yeah, I've got my problems, I'm a work in progress. Kind of like that song "Unforgettable." So many people are bland and interchangeable, but let me tell you, when my friends encounter me, their faces show it. They go pale and shudder with excitement.

Up ahead, flashing red and blue lights outside my place, which reminds me how much I love sleeping on the beach. You know, the smell of the sea and all that rotting dead stuff covered in flies. I have insomnia bad, but if I drink enough NyQuil, the mermaids and mermen come ashore and whisper me bedtime stories.

It's late February, 2020, and this upcoming year looks to be truly magical. I know; I'm an empath and shit. Hope I run into you soon. Bound to happen in a small town. Hey, gotta bounce. Now!

DESTROY ME GENTLY, PLEASE

Evan Burton shut his book in bed to stare over at Rebecca. She wore reading glasses while studying an article in a magazine that he could smell was *Vanity Fair*.

She glanced up. "Do you need to sleep now?"

"No." Evan smiled. "You looked so serious, like a librarian, that's all."

"Uh-huh." Rebecca's mouth twitched as she went back to her article.

Evan wanted to share a vivid scene in *Tree of Smoke* by Denis Johnson but restrained himself. Hearing something from a Vietnam War novel would trouble her dreams. After ten years of marriage, Evan considered Rebecca somewhat fragile, like a sensitive university professor shell-shocked from departmental intrigues and combative students.

The years following the election had been traumatic for both of them. While Evan coped through SNL skits and *The New Yorker* cartoons, Rebecca said, "I can't stand to hear his voice. No more CNN, MSNBC, and especially Fox News." They cut the cable and streamed their shows through a Roku. Despite that, a gloom hung in the air, a despair that couldn't quite be articulated, or dispelled.

"Okay, I'm done." Rebecca switched off her lamp and slipped into the bathroom.

Evan assumed she would brush and floss, then perform the before bed facial rituals most cosmopolitan women did at night, as opposed to their morning facial rituals. His knowledge, and perhaps curiosity, ended there. For although Evan knew his wife intimately—the freckles on her shoulders, the mole on her back and stomach, the wisps of soft brown hair that descended in front of her ears—there were a vast amount of details he would never know. Evan accepted this. Ten years together had created routines: repetitions of conversations, similar arguments, identical silences. Complete knowledge could only exacerbate the side-effect of boredom that came with the stability and beneficial order of marriage.

When Rebecca climbed back in bed, face aglow with a waxy moisturizer, and turned on her side to sleep, Evan kissed the nape of her neck.

She inched away. "Night."

It was Monday, not Thursday. With her museum work, as well as painting, and Evan's copywriting job, his male drinking buddies, and the historical novel that hadn't progressed beyond a thirty-page introduction, they scheduled a weekly date night. Thursday. So he let the Manhattan traffic symphony of diesel horns, car alarms, and ambulance sirens lull him to sleep.

Evan returned after work to their two-bedroom, walk-up apartment on 10th Street between First and Avenue A. Neighbors walked dogs while couples ambled with small children in tow. Evan first experienced the East Village in 1990 as a Columbia freshman. The neighborhood didn't seem livable back when dealers sold drugs openly on stoops in Alphabet City, when condemned buildings had squatters camped inside. Those who rented apartments around Tompkins Square were artists, musicians, and freaks whose greatest creation was themselves.

Now, the East Village had become just another expensive, residential area of Manhattan, bustling with prosperous young families. Upscale bars and restaurants sprouted everywhere.

Each month, Evan signed his rent check in shock over the staggering amount, and imagined the rest of America—save San Francisco—laughing at him.

He tapped on Rebecca's studio door. Norah Jones mellow music sounded. "Hon, I'm going to that vodka account party." He paused. "Do you, uh, want to come?"

"Go ahead," she replied. "I'm in the zone."

Evan rarely ventured inside. Rebecca specialized in still lifes of tables with flowers, fruit and wine glasses. He believed in her talent, but still lifes bored him. In museums, he hurried past them, for they seemed an exercise, not a finished work to be displayed in public. However, even in unguarded moments, Evan never voiced his opinion. Their marriage—and perhaps many others—relied on little lies and deliberate silences.

At the party on 16th Street and Sixth Avenue, a dark-haired, Italian-looking woman smiled at him across the room. *Andrea?* She held her wine glass up in toast.

Evan's marriage had slid into a trough. He loved Rebecca and didn't yearn for random hookups, but missed the flirtation, the chase of his bachelor years. Wanting someone and them wanting you. At least that involved intrigue, a chance to put on your best face, suck in your gut, and stand tall. More electric, more alive than sprawling across the couch in pajamas to watch *Ozark* while munching on popcorn.

After glad-handing clients and chatting up his boss, Evan navigated past guests talking projected sales figures and revenue enhancement. "Good to see you again. Andrea?"

"Angelica." She smirked. "Glad I made an impression."

He laughed.

"Your drink looks like slush, Evan," she said. "You need a fresh one."

"Well, I usually... Maybe you're right."

"Of course I'm right." Angelica's gleaming white teeth emerged between glossed scarlet lips.

After snagging another drink and after Angelica squeezed his arm, Evan said, "You know, we're both involved in this account. Shouldn't I have contact information in case we might help each other?"

"Business goes so much better with collaboration." Angelica pressed her card into his jacket's breast pocket. "Text me when something comes up." Her brown eyes widened.

"Definitely. I have to leave now."

"No reason for me to stay at this dull soiree. Can I join?"

Evan hadn't expected such rapid escalation. "Sorry."

He displayed his wedding ring. "Commitments can be restricting."

"Restricted relationships have benefits too," Angelica said. "You know how to reach me." She stroked his chin with her finger then marched to the bar and began talking to a tall black man in a suit.

Evan tossed her card in a trash can on Sixth Avenue. Tonight's little game had been an ego boost, but he never intended to call Angelica, or any woman. Nor would he bring their cards home to be discovered by accident.

Evan walked to 14th Street to catch the L Train to First Avenue. At the corner, he spied a vendor wheeling a cart and something smelled delicious. Dripping cooked meat encased in melted cheese on a grease-soaked bun. Everything about it was wrong. Horrible. Toxic. Rebecca helped in maintaining Evan's diet, which allowed chicken or turkey, but frowned on beef, much less this sweaty, gray-brown slab of mystery meat. Normally, Evan would have passed it by, however, the second drink had loosened him up. Flirting with no follow-through left an aching void, a desire to break rules, to be bad.

He devoured the glistening sandwich in its paper wrap. The taste was incredible following the finger food at the party. Only after the subway ride did the concoction hit his intestines like a depth charge. "Minor food poisoning," Evan told Rebecca as he rushed to take turns squatting then standing jackknifed over the bowl inside their bathroom.

"Did you break your diet vows?" she asked from outside.

"I blew it. I'm sorry." Wallowing in food guilt felt better than flirtation remorse.

"Don't apologize to me," Rebecca said. "You let yourself down." She paused. "But maybe sleep on the couch, just in case."

On Wednesday nights, Evan met with his old buddies: two married, one perpetually single. They visited favorite local bars without suffering long waits. Between Thursday and Sunday afternoon, the East Village became overrun with students and twenty-somethings. And not just from NYU. Every college in Manhattan, Queens, and Long Island sent their best and brightest down to what they considered a binge-drinking theme park. Doing anything in the neighborhood became impossible.

Evan knocked on Rebecca's studio at eight. A falsetto voice sang from her Pandora feed. Bon Iver, maybe. "Honey?" He tried the door. "You there?"

Rustling sounded. "Just a second." She eventually unlatched the door. "Heading out?"

"You lock your studio now?" He stepped inside. A canvas sat on an easel by a still life table and several stretched canvases stood facing the wall. Artists never liked their work judged in progress. Tarps covered the floor and another lay across her desk.

"Didn't know you were still around," Rebecca replied. "I get nervous here alone. If someone broke in, I could climb out my window onto the fire escape."

"Sure." Evan stared at her current painting. "Thought I saw this three months ago. Seems pretty dry."

She gave him a funny look. "Acrylic paint dries super-fast. That other piece had a blue background, this one's blue-gray."

"Yeah, you're right." He rubbed her shoulder. "Be back by ten."

"Seriously," Rebecca said, "watch the greasy foods."

Evan met Tom and Chris by the secret telephone booth entrance to Please Don't Tell speakeasy. A cluster of people milled about, Manhattan's winter gusting all around them.

"Ninety-fucking-minute wait," Tom said. "This place was really cool three years ago." He touched his graying beard. "Now it's so touristy." A young Chinese couple in line glared at him.

The men walked onto 8th Street and headed downtown. "Where's Andrew?" Evan asked.

"He canceled," Chris replied, his stocky body encased in a down jacket. "Had an online date." His face sagged. "I feel bad for single people."

"Is marriage that much better?" Tom pressed his dark hair back.

"No, but there's consistency."

"Consistency of what?"

"I don't know," Chris answered. "But you have a shared history, and married men live longer statistically."

"Our wives must love that," Evan said.

At the entrance to Death & Company on 6th Street, the doorman ushered the trio inside. A vacated and messy table in the corner magnetized them over before any competition snagged it. They soon ordered a round of ridiculously expensive cocktails.

Chris admitted to watching Internet porn, which peaked on Tuesday nights while his wife attended her book club. This coincided with learning how to delete his browser history.

Tom mentioned that two years after the birth of their second child, he and his wife had sex on a monthly basis.

Evan regaled them with his card-gathering adventures.

"Seems pretty lame," Chris said between sipping his Maker's Mark. "So you get their cards, wow! But you don't know if anything would've happened. Maybe they were networking."

"Sounds like those losers who *friend* old girlfriends on Facebook thinking there's a chance for some reunion nookie." Tom chuckled, but cut it short when his companions maintained a grim silence.

"No one uses nookie anymore," Chris finally said. "Who are you, Rodney Dangerfield?"

"Yeah, but I didn't want to actually score," Evan insisted. "I just wanted..." he lowered his voice, "to be desired."

Two acne-faced young guys at the next table momentarily stopped arguing in Russian and turned with sympathetic curiosity.

"I feel invisible," Evan continued. "Women don't even look at me when I walk by anymore."

"Listen," Chris said, scooping beer nuts. "There's this game, Adult Chicken. You take a woman out and see how close you can get. Ladies are more selective." They laughed. "So they might stop things on the first date, then you win. If they don't stop, then you make an excuse, chicken out and lose." He grinned. "But actually you win. Because you didn't cheat on your wife, and you know you were wanted."

"That's crazy," Evan said, but Googled adult chicken on his iPhone. Images of grown chickens showed, and links to adult cases of chickenpox, but nothing about dating games. "Doesn't exist." He tilted his glowing screen toward them.

Chris sighed. "It's not a thing yet. Adult Chicken isn't the official name. But it sounds better than your stupid getting-business-cards deal." He finished his whiskey. "Hell, I don't need it. Been married three years—"

"In your third marriage."

"With your Internet porn."

"Whatever..." Chris signaled to a server in a bow tie and suspenders for another round.

"I need to get home," Evan said later. "Rebecca gets nervous alone in our apartment."

Date night passed quietly. When Evan and Rebecca pressed together beneath the sheets it was not with animal abandon but more a polite ballet. The event serving as a relaxant before sleep, like taking Unisom or drinking warmed milk.

The following Tuesday, Evan went solo to a party at Empire Merchants in Brooklyn, a wine distributor considering an ad campaign. Once he'd finished schmoozing the owner and managers, Evan approached an attractive wine server. She looked thirtyish, with a bohemian air disguised under a white button-down shirt and black slacks.

"Hate these events," he said. "Everyone acts nice because they want something."

"Don't you want something, from me?"

"Am I being that obvious?"

"I mean, you want more wine," she said. "And if you compliment me, I might pour you a big glass." She half-smiled. "People come to these deals to get buzzed on free wine, then cab over to Peter Luger Steakhouse."

"Not me, and I'd never flatter you," he said and she winced. "That's for trophy wives and the insecure. You're smart and read books, no, graphic novels. Your older brother or last boyfriend got you into eighties music, The Cure and The Smiths, and you can't believe you only just discovered the Velvet Underground, or was it Nina Simone? Your gig here is just so you can paint, or sing, or direct short films."

She laughed. "That's part true."

"Which part?"

"You'll have to find out. What's your name?"

"Uh, Richard..."

She turned, noticing other partygoers approaching for a refill. "Stephanie, and I'm done in a half-hour."

Later, they nestled together in a nearby dive bar's back booth. "I'd like to see the graphic novel you're working on," Evan said.

"It's at my apartment." Stephanie flashed a knowing smile. "Over in Williamsburg. You going to pay for the Uber?"

"Of course. By Metropolitan?"

"Close, why?"

"I live in the East Village," he said, "near the L Train."

Stephanie tried to kiss him during the ride, but Evan demurred, not wanting lipstick or her scent on him. "I'm old-fashioned."

"No, just old." She ran a hand through his hair. "I mean older than me, but I don't have a daddy thing, you know."

Stephanie tensed-up when they climbed to her building's third floor landing. A television blasted sports from inside her apartment. "Listen, I'm sorry, but my roommate's home early."

"I won't scare her."

Stephanie looked stone cold sober, suddenly aged. "It's a *him*." She stood by her door, barring the way. "We, uh, just broke up, but rents are so high we still live... Anyway, it's complicated. I have to say goodnight now, Richard."

"Wait, are you playing the game too?"

Stephanie's face showed confusion. "What game?" She shoved him. "Was this just a stupid joke, pretending to be interested?"

"No, I—"

"Is that you, Steph?" a hoarse voice asked through the door. Locks began to click open.

Evan bolted down the stairs but overheard the man. "You okay? Who was that?"

"The Uber driver," she said. "Some creepy old guy."

Evan rode the L Train to First Avenue and walked south. A ping sounded. He pulled out his iPhone. *You never texted, so I did. Angelica.*

Evan skipped Wednesday guys' night out to meet Angelica. Initially, he'd assumed she liked him, but sounded all business when they spoke by phone.

"I wanted to discuss the account," Angelica said, "and copywriting opportunities for you."

They met at Blue Smoke on 26th Street. Evan talked and talked, company business jabber vomiting out of him. Angelica didn't widen her eyes, smile with bared teeth, or touch his hand. Signals Evan remembered from *Rituals of Seduction*, a book he studied during his bachelor days.

Outside, Evan debated whether to catch the bus or grab the downtown local on Park Avenue.

"I'd love to share some ad ideas," Angelica said. "My office is right around the corner."

"I should get home."

"Fifteen minutes."

They entered a small building and took the elevator to the sixth floor. Angelica opened a door with her key.

"This isn't an office."

"Home office." Angelica surprised Evan, kissing him on the lips. "I think we've covered our business," she said. "Relax on the sofa. I'll change, then fix us a drink."

Evan sat down trembling. *Leave.* Yes, he would lose the game, but enough already. Angelica desired him and his marriage remained uncompromised.

"Bacardi, right?" Angelica appeared in a one-piece, black mesh, see-through number.

Jesus. Evan jumped up. "Sorry, I have to get back to my wife."

"Just stay awhile." She blinked her long lashes. "You know you're interested."

Evan wracked his brain for an excuse. "I didn't take a pill. I can't, you know, without medication."

"No problem." She padded barefoot to the kitchen.

Evan tip-toed toward her front door.

Angelica returned with a jar of brown capsules. "I found these at Organic Health Pharmacy. They kept a seventy-year-old man going last year."

"Wait, what?" Evan felt blindsided over her advance preparation and vaguely disgusted. "No. I'm leaving." He dashed for the elevator. *Where the hell were the fire stairs?*

"You asshole," Angelica yelled from outside her apartment. "You led me on." She threw a stiletto-heeled boot that clanked against the elevator door. "This isn't over."

Neighbors' voices sounded, but thankfully the elevator arrived and Evan escaped. He trekked home on foot in the brisk March weather to calm his ratcheting heart. Everything returned to normal once safe inside his apartment. Rebecca painted in her studio and he watched an episode of *Black Mirror* on Netflix.

"How were the guys?" Rebecca asked as they fell asleep spooning.

"Who? Oh, the same."

"No greasy meats?"

"Never again."

She laughed. "Night."

Evan's boss called him into his office at ten a.m. "Someone from the vodka account wants to drop us because of your ad copy." Gerald Murphy worried a hand through his curly red hair. "I said you'd rewrite it, a complete do-over, but got nowhere." He waved a piece of paper. "Here's her number. Handle this."

Gravity pressed down when Evan saw the familiar digits. "I'll get on it right away."

Back in his cubicle, Evan rested his head on his desk. He was done. Game over. Marriage may have lost its excitement, his wife might be a tender soul, extra-sensitive, and unsuited for the harsh city, but they had something. A union. Shared beliefs. Even an economic dependency caused by astronomical Manhattan rents. He heard a ping and shuddered. *Call me.* Rebecca never contacted him at work.

"What's up, honey?" Evan asked minutes later.

"I'm at the museum." Rebecca worked at MOMA in the archives' holdings department. "This woman Angelica who does business with you called. Asked to meet me tomorrow. She claimed it was urgent, about our financial situation."

"That's insane." Evan struggled to maintain a steady voice.

"She mentioned you were playing something. Evan, you still there? I didn't understand. Have you been gambling?"

"No," he said, face drooping. "I'm not sure you should—"

"I agreed to do lunch with her tomorrow. Anyway, have to dash. See you later."

Evan hid until five, then crept toward the elevator.

Murphy lunged from his office. "Did you clear everything up?"

"I'll rework the copy tonight." Evan smiled. "It'll be settled by tomorrow afternoon."

"Let's hope so." Murphy frowned and retreated.

Evan texted Rebecca. *Can we postpone date night? My boss wants to review accounts.*

No problem, she replied. *When are you coming home?*

By ten. Love you.

Evan cloistered himself at Nuclear Burger, a loud, bright joint on the corner of 14th Street. It symbolized everything wrong with the new East Village. Overpriced and impersonal, a waiting lounge where Gen Z and millennials sat texting before venturing to wherever the real party was.

Evan barely tasted his turkey burger. He lingered, yet still departed before nine. Time to confess; break it gently and head off Angelica's information dump. Rebecca wouldn't throw him out, but tears and depression could follow. Their date night taken off the calendar for God knows how long. Her mother was South American, bold and brusque, but Rebecca seemed so delicate. A Mediterranean woman would just slap his face, spit on him, and yell, *"Bastardo!"* But not internalize, not shrink into herself and slowly wither away.

He opened their front door. Dissonant music blasted down the foyer from the living room. Evan recognized his old Sonic Youth CD. Rebecca's studio door hung wide open and she sang along. "The song I hate..."

Evan lowered the stereo's volume.

"You're back early."

He stood in her doorway facing the floor. "I'm sorry, I screwed up," he started. "I was bored. It's just a game, to flirt with women. Never went through with it, never cheated. Angelica wanted to tell you, but I swear, nothing happened between us."

"Yeah, I know." Rebecca collected her brushes, seeming indifferent to his speech. When she took dirty paint water to dump in the utility bathroom, Evan advanced inside.

Canvases previously hidden under tarps were now displayed. One showed a nude female couple with tattoos kissing, another featured a naked Latino man smiling defiantly. *Their superintendent, Victor?* Books on philosophy, Pagan witchcraft, and feminist pornography lay scattered around. A half-burned joint smoldered in an ashtray.

Evan took a deep breath. Ten years together with a Rebecca he'd created in his mind. A connect-the-dots image that suited his reality, his vanity. His truth, not hers. The stranger he married emerged from the bathroom, hair messy and wild, face flushed. She wore paint-spattered jeans and a tank top. "I'm sorry," he said.

"Stop apologizing."

"It was the game..."

"Chicken for Adults." Rebecca smirked.

"You know about it?"

"Sure." She sighed. "I played it six months ago." Rebecca's expression showed infinite annoyance. "We're way beyond that now."

Evan recoiled and rushed outside—as if he'd forgotten something, as if he'd mistakenly entered the wrong building. He wandered south through an East Village no longer familiar, a bitter headwind piercing him as swollen gray clouds overhead promised messy weather. Neighbors' features blurred while his body went numb; Evan's cheeks stung from the cold and his eyes teared up.

At Bleeker Street and Bowery, Evan confronted the John Varvatos and Patagonia stores where CBGB had once been a landmark, a musical hub. That club represented everything dirty and wild and free about downtown Manhattan. He suddenly felt like a time traveler marooned in an era that held nothing for him. Snow descended and the wind blew wet flakes against his face. Instinctively, he flagged a yellow cab. After ducking into the cloistered warmth of the back seat, he defrosted in silence. The driver's head turned, waiting for an address, the taxi idling by the curb.

Evan didn't have the vaguest notion of where he wanted to go.

AFTERWORD

I'd like to thank my treasured writer friends from our former group: Nick, Rick, Maryanne, Jack, and of course Stephen, for hearing most of these stories. Their enthusiasm and detailed comments helped me go beyond what I blindly assumed were finished pieces. Also, thanks to Genna of *The Opiate*, and the editors at literary journals who first published many of the stories in this volume. Their belief among a blizzard of rejections was sustaining. I'll dedicate this book to my two sisters, Marina and Melanie, and my cousin-in-law, Milda. To have the council of super-intelligent and funny women is a blessing, despite my odd tendency to move thousands of miles away from them.

ABOUT THE AUTHOR

Max Talley is a writer and an artist from New York City who lives in Southern California. He graduated from a liberal arts college in Vermont and was in bands that performed at CBGB and Bleeker Street clubs. Talley has two published novels, two short story collections, and a hippie crime novel, *Peace, Love, & Haight*, forthcoming from Three Rooms Press. Over sixty stories and essays of Talley's have appeared in literary journals from *The Opiate* to *The Saturday Evening Post*. He teaches annual writing workshops at Santa Barbara Writers Conference, at Santa Fe Workshops, and in private homes. Learn more here: www.maxtalley.com